# SHELBY REEVES

Healing the *Pieces*

*Happy reading!*
*Shelby*

# *Healing the Pieces*

*Book 2 in the Pieces Series*

Copyright 2015 by Shelby Reeves

Photography by Lindee Robinson Photography

Cover Design by Danielle Styles

Interior Design and Formatting by T.J. Tims

## Dedication

To everyone who took a chance on a new author and wanted more. This is for you. Thank you!

# Acknowledgments

To my amazing readers who fell in love with Adam and Kaylee in book one, thank you for taking a chance on a new author. Book two would not be possible without your love and support!

To my husband, who I love more than life. I'm truly blessed to have you as my soulmate!

My parents- Thank you for loving me and being there for me.

Mary Lynn and Kaela, my sisters from another mother, I love you girls so much! Mary Lynn you have supporting me from the very beginning when I told you I wanted to write a novel. Kaela, you need to move your butt to Alabama! Oh, and thanks for loving me and supporting me through this journey!

My best friends- You girls know who you are without having to name each and every one of you. You girls rock! I love y'all!

Shannon- Girl I don't even know where to start with how awesome you are! I love our conversations and I can't wait to hug you in person! Love ya bunches!

To the fellow authors who have helped me and given me advice...Thank you!

To all the blogs that have shared my author page, teasers, and helped promote me...Thank you for helping me get my name out in the book world.

#  Prologue

A gunshot rings out, freezing time momentarily while my breathing stops completely. Moments ago, I murmured a quick prayer for all of us as I watched the gun raise and point in my direction. I stand, in shock, gaping at this person before me. My hand covers my mouth as I choke back a sob. It rips through my throat regardless, letting a painful cry escape. *This can't be happening,* I think to myself over and over. I get one problem taken care of then another happens. I thought I knew who was behind the threats. Boy…was I wrong. I was certain it was Riley, but this person before me is not him. I never expected this person to be the *main* source of my problems.

"Kaylee…" Alexis' voice trembles next to me. Her hand is clutching mine so tight that it's numb, but I can't imagine I would feel it anyway. My whole body is numb as I stare at the person who is holding my life in the palm of their hand. One shot and my fate is sealed. One shot and my babies will not have a chance at life. One shot and I will be taken away from the one person I can't live without. *Adam.* You hear stories about how a person's life flashes before their eyes all the time. That's what's happening to me right now. Adam's charming smile is the last thing I see before a black blur clouds my vision for a brief, horrifying second.

"Alexis, no!" But it was too late. I drop to the floor to aid my best friend. I am screaming so loudly, my voice is cracking. "ALEXIS!"

Elizabeth laughs wickedly, and I snap my head up to see her raise the gun for a second time. "Tell your father I love him for me." I squeeze my eyes shut and wait for the ringing of the gun and the pain to follow. I hug my belly, praying that my babies and my best friend make it out alive.

*Kaylee*

*"I hate this. I hate what I've become, and more than anything, I hate that there is no way out."-Riley*

My mother.

The threat.

The trial.

I have all these things happening in my life that I can't stop. I want so badly for all of this to disappear. Maybe then, my life would finally be normal. Well, as normal as it can be without my father. His letter gives me a little closure but not much. I would scream until my lungs are sore if I knew it would erase all of the bad things happening right now. I would scream until I don't have a voice anymore. Too bad life doesn't work like that.

Reuniting with Ethan.

Adam's unconditional love for me.

My unborn babies.

The support I get from Adam's parents and Alexis.

They all keep me from going insane. If Dad was here, he would say something like, "Don't you worry your pretty little head, Kaylee. I promise it will be over soon." He would then kiss my hair and tell me that he loves me. Dad was always positive about things, no matter the situation. I wish I could be more hopeful like he was.

Having Ethan back in my life is helping me deal with things. Our bond is stronger than ever before. I am thankful that he reached out to me. If it wasn't for him wanting to resolve the wedge between us, who knows how long it would've been before we reconciled.

Adam. Where do I begin with him? He is my rock, my greatest supporter. I cannot be more thankful that my car didn't start the night of the back to school party. He has stayed by my side through things that normally would tear couples apart. Because of him, I have hope. Because of him, I am healing. At times, I reflect on my life before him and wonder how I ever made it.

I'm so blessed to have Anna and Jack in my life. No one will ever replace my father or his memory, but Anna can definitely take my mother's place. Growing up, I had it all. My father cherished me and spoiled me to no end. I had everything I could ever want before it was all ripped away from me. Now, my mom has become someone I don't recognize, and my dad is just a memory—someone I loved dearly, but someone I'll never see again.

Alexis has been my best friend through thick and thin. She is always there to provide a shoulder to lean on when I need a good cry. She also knows when I need a good laugh because she always does something that causes me to laugh.

The prospect of becoming a mother has finally stopped scaring me. Mostly, I'm nervous, but I know with everyone's help, especially Adam's, I will be okay. I'm starting to feel little flutters in my stomach, kind of like butterflies, which feels surreal. On the downside, my clothes are getting pretty tight. I foresee a trip to the mall real soon for some yoga pants and oversized t-shirts. I've been putting it off because it bothers me that Adam and his family, even Alexis and her family, pay for my things. I know they say that they want to, but I still feel as if I'm mooching off them.

I had planned to talk to Ethan about staying with Adam again, but now that is far from my mind. The note flashes in front of me once more. The red block letters against the white parchment mock me. I curl my body closer to Adam's and sigh. We haven't moved from the couch since seeing the letter. Ethan has just been sitting in the recliner across from us, staring down at the floor. I want to go hug my brother. I don't like seeing him hurt because of me, but I don't want to move out of Adam's safe embrace.

"I know what you're thinking, sweetheart, and I promise you that nothing is going to happen to you." He has been telling me this nonstop since I jumped back into his arms. I wish I could believe him when he tells me that. "I'll keep you safe. Do you trust me?" I do trust him; I'm just having a moment of self-doubt.

I lift my head off his chest and stare into his deep blue eyes. "I trust you, Adam, with all my heart. I'm just scared that something is going to happen to someone I love again. I can't go through that a second time. I'm still dealing with my father's death. If I lose…if I lose someone else, I don't think I'll ever recover." The pain I felt, and still feel, from losing the person I was closest to is something I never want to experience again.

Adam leans in and presses his lips to mine. He kisses me slowly, reassuringly. I melt against him, relishing the feel of his comfort. When he pulls away, he drops his hand to my barely rounded stomach. "Our babies need you to be healthy for them. Stressing out and worrying is not healthy for you or them. Let me deal with the note and you just worry about taking care of yourself, okay?" My heart swells when I hear him say "our babies." I don't like the idea of Adam dealing with my problems, but I know he is right. I have to think about more than myself now.

I place my hands over his that are lying across my belly and nod in agreement. "Just promise me that you'll be careful."

"I promise, sweetheart."

My eyes drift back to Ethan, who still hasn't moved at all. If I couldn't see that he was breathing, I would have thought he was dead. That is how still and silent he is.

Adam nudges me so I angle my head and give him a questioning look. He just nods his head in Ethan's direction, silently communicating for me to go comfort him. I gingerly climb out of Adam's hold and walk over to Ethan. I place my hand on his shoulder, and he responds by pulling me in for a hug. Neither of us says anything. If he wants to say something, I'll let him speak first.

"I can't lose you, sis. I just got you back," he cries on my shoulder. He suddenly breaks our hug and looks me straight in my eyes. Determination is written all over his face. "I will find out who is doing this, and I will make them pay." I wanted to debate the whole "make them pay" part, but I just kept my mouth shut. I just want all of this to stop. "Call Alexis and tell her that I am coming to pick her up so that we can discuss this."

"Okay." I stand and walk into the spare room in Ethan's apartment where I have been staying. I grab my phone off the nightstand and dial her number.

"Hey, baby girl. What's up?"

"Ethan is fixing to leave to come pick you up." Silence. "I'll explain when you get here, I promise."

"Okay." She drags out the word. "Hang on a second." I hear muffled voices for a second before she comes back on the line. "Brad said he'll bring me over there." Oh, boy…this may not go well. I tell her to come on and hit end. I set my phone back down on the nightstand before heading back out into the living room.

"Um, Brad said he'll bring her over here," I tell Ethan. He nods stiffly and walks into the kitchen. That went better than I expected it to.

Adam laughs softly. "That went well."

I sigh and plop down next to him on the couch. His arm snakes around my waist. "That's what I thought, too, but they haven't gotten here yet."

"True. My money is on Ethan."

"Adam," I scold.

He shrugs. "What? No offense to Brad, but I never want to piss your brother off."

"Smart guy. I knew I liked him," Ethan chimes in as he walks back into the living room.

A couple of minutes later, there is a knock on the door. I start to get up to answer it, but Ethan motions for me to stay. He looks through the peephole before opening the door and letting Brad and Alexis inside. I didn't miss the scowl on Ethan's face when they walked in hand in hand. Ethan takes a long look outside before stepping back in and closing the door, firmly locking it. Brad and Adam slap hands and Alexis moves to hug me. Brad and Ethan just nod at one another. *Awkward.* Alexis takes the remaining seat on the couch beside me, and Brad moves to lean against the wall.

"Okay, uh…" Ethan claps his hand as he begins. "I had Kaylee call you here so we could all be on the same page. Someone left a note for Kaylee in my mailbox today, and they're just asking for a death wish. I've already told Kaylee not to go anywhere without Adam or me, but it would help if you were involved." He directs the last sentence at Brad, who nods in agreement.

Before either one of them can get a word out, I speak up. "What about Alexis?"

Ethan's eyes flick to my best friend for a brief second before focusing on me. I didn't miss that nor did I miss her tense up beside me. "What about her?"

"Is she not in as much danger as I am for hanging out with me?"

"The threat wasn't directed at her; however, it doesn't mean that whoever it is won't use her to get to you." I want to roll my eyes and say, *my point exactly*, but I refrain from doing so.

"Don't worry about me, baby girl. I can handle my own," Alexis says confidently.

"No, she's right," Brad interjects, causing us of all to look at him. "Lex, even though no threat has been directed toward you, it doesn't mean that you are safe."

Ethan scowls at Brad when he calls her "Lex."

I want to yell; I want to close my eyes and wish this nightmare away. I don't want anything to happen to anyone else because of me. I can't let it happen.

"The same rules apply to you," Ethan says, staring directly at my best friend. "Don't leave the house, school, anywhere without Adam, Brad, or me. Neither of you should be anywhere by yourselves and that includes being at home, too. Not until all this shit is settled."

I turn to my best friend, unable to hide my sadness. "I'm sorry, Alexis. I didn't mean to involve you in this," I whisper sadly to her.

She shakes her head. "Don't you dare apologize to me. You're my best friend. Sticking by you is what I'm here for." She gives me a hug, trying to reassure me though it doesn't.

"What did the letter say?" Brad asks.

I shudder when I recollect the content of the letter.

Adam picks up the threatening letter and hands it to Brad. I watch his eyes scan the paper. He curses under his breath and crumples the paper in his hand. "Are we all on the same page as to who we think is behind this?" Another shudder passes through my body when Riley's face flashes in my mind. I close my eyes, lay my head on Adam's shoulder, and move my hand to find his, threading our fingers. I squeeze his hand hard. I'm gripping it so tight that I'm afraid I might break my hand. Adam kisses my hair before laying his head on mine.

Faintly, I hear Adam and Ethan snarl, "Yes." Even I know it has to be Riley.

"But how can he if he is locked up?" Alexis shrieks. I'm wondering the same thing, too.

"Lex, he could have someone doing this for him. There are ways, babe," Brad says. I'm glad I have my eyes closed because I know Ethan is probably killing Brad in his mind since he called her "Lex" and "babe" in the same sentence.

A yawn escapes me before I realize it. "Do you want to go lie down, sweetheart?" Adam whispers in my hair, and I nod my head. I'm tired of discussing what is happening. He kisses my hair once more before standing and walking over to Ethan and Brad.

I turn to my best friend. "I'm going to call it a night. Talk to you tomorrow?"

She leans over and hugs me. "Get some rest, baby girl, and I'll text you later." With one last squeeze, she lets me go. Adam is already back in front of me, holding his hand out for me to take. I place my hand in his and stand. I hug Ethan and tell him that I love him before walking over to Brad. I give him a quick hug and thank him for being here for me.

Hopefully, I will be able to sleep tonight though I have an eerie feeling that a nightmare will make its presence once I'm asleep. At least Adam will be here to help me through it even though I hate it when he sees me like that. I don't even bother changing into my pajamas, and I just climb into bed. Adam lays down beside me and pulls me close. I relax some, but the weight of the threat is still there. "I don't think I'll be able to sleep tonight, Adam," I admit softly.

He turns on his side and cups my face. "Relax, Kaylee. Take a deep breath and listen to me." I take a deep breath as he says, "You are safe. No one will get to you, I swear." His piercing blue eyes gaze deep into my frightened ones. "I love you so much, sweetheart." His hand leaves my face and drops to my belly. "And I love them, too."

"I love you, too, Adam. It would kill me if I lost you."

"Ditto, sweetheart, but neither of us is going to lose one another, ever." I grab the back of his neck and lower his face to mine. His lips touch mine tenderly, melting my insides into a pool of want. Adam kisses me once more before pulling away. I lay my head against his chest and sigh, feeling content.

"Dream of me, sweetheart."

I mumble some sort of agreement and drift off to sleep with Adam and his kisses on my mind.

## 2

*Adam*

*"Seeing that Adam makes her happy, makes me feel...relieved."- Riley*

Once Kaylee is fast asleep, I slip out of bed and walk back into the living room where Ethan, Brad, and Alexis are all sitting. An uncomfortable silence blankets the room. I need to hurry up and talk to Ethan before Kaylee wakes up and needs me. I want to be holding her the moment a nightmare creeps in. With the threat and the mention of Riley's name, it's likely she'll need me tonight. Brad and Alexis are sitting side by side on the couch. Brad has his arm around her shoulders. Ethan is staring hard at Brad, who doesn't seem bothered by it.

Ethan finally pulls his attention away from Brad and looks at me.

"I wanted to talk to you quickly about Kaylee staying with me again."

He sits quietly, obviously thinking long and hard about it. I know he doesn't like the idea of her living with me. He made that apparent from the day we met. I've already got my argument prepared for when he says no. I'm sure I'll need it.

"I don't know, man." Well, that is better than a flat out no. "I just got my sister back. I'm not sure if I am ready to give her up again."

"It's not like I am going to keep her from you. You're welcome to come see her anytime or vice versa."

Sadness fills his eyes. "You don't understand, Adam. I have four years to make up. I should have tried harder to see her. Maybe all this wouldn't be happening if I had." I know how he feels because I feel like I am partly to blame for what Riley did to her. If I had seen what he had been doing all along, I could have stopped it.

"We are all to blame, Ethan. Not just you," Alexis says, sorrow dripping from her words.

Before I can say anything, Brad speaks up. "I'm sorry, Lex, but I don't agree with that statement. The only person responsible is Riley; *he* did this. Not any of us sitting in this room right now, but Riley…he is to blame for every bruise, nightmare…everything. You all need to stop taking the blame from who it rightfully belongs to." The room is now quiet again as we all let Brad's words sink in. In hindsight, we know he is right, but it is tough knowing you could have stopped it and did nothing.

After a couple of minutes of silence, Ethan is the first to speak. "I feel like I won't be able to protect her at all if she stays with you. You will be with her during the day at school, and if she stays with you, at night. When will I get a chance to protect her? I won't be able to sleep knowing she's not here."

"It goes both ways, Ethan. I won't be able to sleep knowing she's here and not with me, either. What if she has a nightmare and you can't stop it?"

Ethan scrubs his face with his hands, clearly unsure what to do.

"Here's a thought. Why don't you boneheads let her decide?" Alexis says with disgust. "Kaylee needs to make the decision she's most comfortable with and you both will just have to deal with it." Alexis stands suddenly and turns to Brad. "You ready?" He nods and gets up off the couch. "I hope that you will let her make the decision. God knows that enough of her choices have been taken from her." Alexis walks to the front door without another word. Brad mutters a quick good-bye to me and gives Ethan a hard nod before running to catch up with Alexis.

"We'll talk to Kaylee in the morning." Ethan nods, and I turn to make my way back to my sleeping beauty. I spent way more time away from her than I needed to. I open the door and close it quietly behind me. I unbutton my jeans and let them fall to the floor. Once I kick them off, I peel off my shirt and discard it with my pants. By the time I reach the bed, she has already turned twice in her sleep. She's getting restless. I quickly crawl in beside her and wrap my arms around her, silently letting her know that I am here. She immediately drapes her arm over my stomach and her body relaxes automatically. This, among other reasons, is why I don't want her to stay here. If she chooses to, then I'll respect her decision and try to be okay with it. I just hope that Ethan doesn't throw a fit if she chooses to come back with me. I know it will be a tough decision for her. Hopefully, there is a solution that all three of us will be okay with.

Morning comes too soon for my liking. I don't want to unwrap my arms from her nor do I want to hear her say she wants to stay here. My parents won't let me stay here every night; I know that for a fact. If it weren't for someone threatening Kaylee, I wouldn't even be here right now. It's not that I have anything against Ethan, it's just…when she's with me, *I* know she is safe. I'm sure he feels the same way. I do trust Ethan, don't get me wrong, but if she's with him, I will be constantly worrying about her and our little unborn babies.

I feel her stir next to me and whisper my name. "Morning, sweetheart," I say as I bend down to nuzzle her neck.

"Morning," she grumbles, and I hold back my snicker. She isn't a morning person…at all. Too bad for her, I am.

"Why don't you rest while I go fix you some breakfast?"

"Whatever," she grumbles and rolls away from me. I drop a kiss on her forehead and throw on my clothes before heading to the kitchen to find something for her to eat. Ethan is already up and leaning against the kitchen counter drinking coffee. I head straight for the fridge and pull out the eggs, bacon, and biscuits. Once I preheat and butter the biscuits, I place them in the oven and set the timer.

"Everything go all right during the night?" Ethan asks. What he is really asking is, "Did she have a nightmare?"

"When I first walked in, I noticed her tossing and turning a little, but as soon as I wrapped my arms around her, she relaxed and slept through the night."

He looks down at the coffee mug in his hand and sighs heavily. "I hate that she's going through this."

"I tell her all the time how strong she is despite all the things she's been through." Kaylee blows me away with her strength and her refusal to give up.

"Kaylee has always been that way." He chuckles as if he was thinking of something funny. "I remember one day she twisted her ankle really bad. She was six or so at the time, and I remember thinking it had to be broken. She was trying her hardest not to cry and to be tough. Even while the doctor examined it and had her try and walk on it, she held the tears in like a champ." He laughs softly at the memory. "Later that day, I told her I was surprised she didn't shed a tear. Kaylee looked at me with a straight face and said, "I wanted people to see I was as strong as my bubba.""

"You two were really close, huh?" Kaylee has told me a couple of times that they were closer than most siblings were and how she missed it.

"Yeah, we were like two peas in a pod. We hardly ever argued or fought; that's how well we got along. If she ever needed me, then I came running ready to kick someone's ass." We both laugh at that.

"How was her relationship with Elizabeth when she was younger?" I ask as I lay the bacon in the frying pan.

"Okay, I guess. I mean, Elizabeth never abused her if that's what you're asking. Dad would have never allowed it since she was his pride and joy. Obviously, they didn't have a close relationship like she did with Dad. Elizabeth was nice to her, but I always thought it was forced. I think she knew that Dad would boot her ass out if she was rude to Kaylee in the slightest."

"If Kaylee chooses to stay with me, you won't get upset with her, will you? I'll respect her decision if she decides to stay here. I won't like it, but I won't be mad at her." Upsetting her is the last thing she needs, especially since she's pregnant. Kaylee has been upset enough lately. Seeing her cry breaks my heart in two.

Ethan sets his empty mug down on the counter and turns to me. "No, I trust you with her. I know you love her, but like I said last night, I want to make up for lost time."

Ethan and I don't say another word when we see Kaylee entering the kitchen looking half-asleep. "Morning, sweetheart," I say when she reaches me. Her arms go around my waist and she leans her head against my chest.

"Mmm…what are you making?" She pulls her head back and tilts it upward. I drop a kiss on her forehead, then her lips.

"Bacon, eggs, and biscuits."

"Sounds yummy." Her arms leave my waist as she steps back. She then walks over and tells her brother good morning and gives him a hug as well.

The oven sounds, signaling the biscuits have finished. I check to make sure they are done before pulling them out. The bacon has finished as well so I turn off the stove burner and get another pan to start the eggs. I notice that it is quiet other than the noise that I'm making so I chance a look at Ethan and Kaylee and I find that both of them are staring at me with amused looks.

"What?"

"I didn't know you can cook, Adam," Kaylee says with a laugh.

"For you, sweetheart, I'll do anything," I answer honestly because I would. I'm so far gone that if she asked me to jump, I'd answer, "How high?"

Ethan snorts and grabs a piece of bacon. "Kiss ass."

I answer him by flipping him off.

I crack the eggs in the frying pan and start fixing them. Kaylee grabs a plate and starts piling it with bacon and biscuits. "You didn't have to do this, but thank you."

"I know I didn't have to; I wan-what's wrong?" I ask suddenly when her hand shoots up to cover her mouth and she takes off running out of the kitchen. I turn off the burner on the stove and follow Ethan, who is right on her heels.

Sick. My girl is feeling sick. I hand her a damp cloth to clean her face.

"It was the eggs; the smell of them."

"No eggs, got it." Once she brushes her teeth, I make her go lie down on the couch regardless of how many times she tells me that she's fine. I bring Kaylee her plate and a glass of juice.

"I really am fine, Adam," she tells me again for the twentieth time in ten minutes. She sits up with her back against the edge of the couch.

"Humor me, sweetheart. Please."

"I'm going to throw up at times. It's inevitable and part of being pregnant." She's right, but I can't not try. "Thank you again for fixing me breakfast. It is wonderful."

"You're welcome. I'll do it again for you."

"Remember, no eggs."

"Right, no eggs." Ethan clears his throat, and I know it's time for her to choose. "Uh, sweetheart, Ethan and I want to talk to you about something."

Her body automatically locks up like she is preparing for the worst. Fear is evident in her eyes. "Is it bad?"

"No, baby, it's not." She visibly relaxes, and the fear leaves her eyes. I take her empty plate and set it on the coffee table behind me. I take both of her hands in mine and kiss each one. "Your brother and I sort of talked last night about who you would stay with. We decided that we wanted you to choose. Please know that if you choose to stay here, I'll be okay with it." I watch her eyes shift from me to Ethan, and her indecision is clear. I don't want her to think I'll be upset with her for not choosing me.

"I don't know if I can choose between you two. Ethan, you're my brother and I've missed not having you around. Adam, you're my rock. Without you, I don't know if I would've have made it this far." I open my mouth to argue with that statement, but she waves me off. "Give me the day to think about it because this will be a hard decision." She swings her legs off the couch and removes her hands from mine. "I'm going to take a shower and then I need to let your parents know that they no longer have to keep the secret."

What? My eyes practically bug out of their sockets. "Are you saying they knew this whole time?" I ask dumbfounded. Her nod just confirmed it. My parents knew why she left; they knew she was pregnant. "I think it's time for payback."

"Adam…what are you going to do?"

"Just go along with it, okay? Go take a shower." This is going to be the highlight of my day.

## 3

*Adam*

*"Having Kaylee in my arms again feels like home." -Adam*

Kaylee saying she needed the day to think about it was not what I expected her to say. If a day is what she needs, I'll give it to her. Judging by Ethan's expression, it wasn't what he expected her to say either. When I texted Mom yesterday evening, all I told her was that I would be staying with Kaylee and we were going to talk. I didn't elaborate so she has no clue that I know everything now.

Forty-five minutes later, we were on the road home. Mom and Dad have no clue what time we'll arrive, which incidentally, is part of my plan. Ethan is behind us in his truck. Kaylee is next to me, our fingers linked and her head on my shoulder.

When I pull into the driveway, I notice Mom and Dad are both at home. "It's showtime."

"I still don't even know what you're up to. Am I supposed to be doing anything?"

"Just go with it, sweetheart." That's all I tell her before opening my door and climbing out. While Kaylee was in the shower, I told Ethan my plan so he knew how to play his part. It's better to keep Kaylee in the dark or otherwise my parents will know I am faking.

When we walk in, I can hear Mom in the kitchen, baking no doubt. She and Dad are gushing over something, it sounds like. I have a pretty good idea what, and it makes my plan so much sweeter. I'm not mad at them because they were just doing what Kaylee asked them to do. I see Mom stuffing something in her purse the moment she notices we are here.

"Adam, you're home earlier than expected." This is going better than I expected. Mom looks like a kid who just got caught with her hand in the cookie jar.

Pointing to the white envelope sticking out of her purse, I ask, "What's that?"

"Oh, this?" Mom looks so nervous she's starting to sweat. "Uh…" She looks anxiously at Dad.

"I wrote her a love letter, son." Really, Dad? That's all you could come up with?

"Can I read it?"

"Uh, no," Mom says quickly. Too quickly. I had them right where I wanted them.

"Why not?"

"Because it's private. Besides, do you really want to read all the lovey-dovey stuff?"

"Yes, Mom, I do." I'm laughing so hard on the inside watching them squirm.

"How about later, sweetie?"

"How about I tell you that you're lying?" Busted. "What's going on, Mom, Dad? I'm not stupid. I know you are hiding something, and I want to know what it is." Mom's eyes are wide as saucers as she looks between her purse and Kaylee.

Now it's Ethan's turn to join in. "Adam, why don't you just leave it alone, man. If it was something they wanted you to see, they'd show you."

"No, I want to know."

"Uh, sweetie, it's um…" When Mom looks back at Kaylee again, she's practically pleading with Kaylee to speak up or give her the go-ahead.

Okay, I've made her sweat long enough. My lips automatically form a smile. "Chill, Mom, I already know. Good to know you can keep a secret, though."

"What?" she screeches. "Lucas Adam Thomas! Why would you do such a thing? You know you're not too old for me to take over my knee!" The whole room bursts into laughter, except me. I know my mom, and she is serious. Mom walks around from behind the island and bear hugs Kaylee. "I glad you finally told him, sweetie. I wasn't sure how much longer I'd be able to hold it in!" she exclaims. Then Mom's face lights up as she lets go of Kaylee and walks quickly back around the island and produces the envelope from her purse. She hands Kaylee the envelope, who in turn hands it to me.

I open the flap and pull out the small photograph. I study it, mesmerized by the two peanut-size human beings. With the pictures in one hand, I raise my arm and drape it over Kaylee's shoulders. She leans into me and I instinctively press my lips to her temple. How did she feel the moment she found out? I'm sure she was scared. How could she not be? When did she go to the doctor? What all did they tell her? Hell, I don't even know when she is due. I was so caught up in having her back in my arms that I never asked. I need to rectify that, like right now. "I'm going to steal her for just a minute," I blurt out to whoever is listening. My arm falls from her shoulders, and I grasp her hand. Pulling her out of the kitchen, I head straight for my room. The moment the door closes behind her, my mouth is on hers and her back is against the door. The second my tongue thrusts in her mouth, her hands tug on my hair.

I'm fighting an inner battle with myself. I want to continue this, but I need to know some things. I forcibly make myself stop and draw back slightly. Before I say what's on my mind, I take one last look at the ultrasound picture and place it on the nightstand. "I'm an asshole, Kaylee." She stares at me, obviously confused by my outburst. "I was so thrilled that you came back to me and not once have I asked you anything about the pregnancy. Not once have I asked you about the doctor. I mean, I wish you had told me so I could have been there, but still, I should know what's going on. I was just thinking about how it would be hard to be supportive if I have no clue what's happening, ya know? Like when you found out you were pregnant, were you alone? How did you feel? Were you happy, scared? What did you think when you saw the two pink lines or heard the doctor tell you?"

When her eyes start to water, I silently curse myself because upsetting her was not part of my plan. Her hands leave my hair and cup my cheeks. "Adam, you are anything but an asshole. I could go on all day about how amazing you are. To be honest, I didn't think about telling you those things either since we kind of got sidetracked." A mischievous smile appears on her face and I laugh. "Life happened, Adam, and it's okay.

"Your mom and Alexis were with me when I took the test. I had gotten sick again that morning, and your mom thought I should take a test, just to be sure. They held my hand and we closed our eyes and found out together. When I saw the result, I started bawling because the first thought that ran through my mind was how I wasn't sure I could be a mother. The second thought, the one that hurt me the most, was that you were going to leave me. I somehow thought that if I told you, then you would think that I cheated and leave me or you would tell me that you didn't want to take care of a child who isn't biologically yours. The 'cheating' thing was crazy, but the second part, that I believed wholeheartedly."

I should have been there so I could've held her while she cried.

"It was my fault that you believed that, Kaylee. I made you doubt our relationship."

"How do you always turn it around so you're the one to blame? None of it was your fault. Being pregnant and carrying someone else's child is a huge deal."

"It's not like it was intentional, sweetheart. You were forced," I bite out as I cover my hands with hers. "Tell me about your first appointment with the doctor." I listen intently as she tells me every detail—the heartbeat, all of it. When she's done, I waste no time letting her know how in love I am with her. I'm never letting her slip away from me again. "We should get back out there before someone comes and drags us out of here."

She gives me one long, breathtaking kiss before dropping her hands and opening my bedroom door. Momentarily stunned, I stand with my mouth hanging open, just watching her walk out of my room. I shake my head, ridding myself of her spell. I jog down the hall to catch up with her and steal another kiss because I can, just as we reach the kitchen. I hear an "Aww…" from Mom and Alexis while Dad and Ethan just smile. Right on cue, Kaylee blushes. I move to stand behind her so I can wrap my arms around her waist. She leans back in my embrace and covers my arms with hers.

I hope to hell that she chooses to stay with me.

I know I said I'd respect her decision, but that doesn't mean I won't try to sway her just a bit.

My phone vibrates in my pocket, startling me. I pull it out and instantly frown when I see it's Ryder. I have a sick feeling he is about to tell me something bad. I excuse myself and walk away. I slide my finger across the screen, answering the call.

"Hello," I say into the phone when it reaches my ear.

"Good morning, Mr. Thomas. I'm afraid I have some bad news." Figures. "I've just received word that once again Mr. Thompson's bail has been posted. He left our facilities yesterday evening. I'm sorry you're just now finding out, but as I said, I just learned of the news myself."

"Who in their damn mind would post his bail? They are basically letting him walk free!" I can't believe this shit. Obviously, he was the one who left the note in Ethan's mailbox for Kaylee. I tell Ryder so and he tells me to bring it to his office so he can send it off and check it for fingerprints. My blood is still raging when I hang up with the detective. I take a few deep breaths, trying to calm myself before I walk back in to face my family. I need to take a drive somewhere real quick, and I need Ethan to go with to make sure I don't do something stupid. Everyone's heads turn in my direction when I walk back in. They are all looking at me questionably.

I ignore everyone's look, but one. "Hey sweetheart, I need to run an errand real quick and I need your brother to go with. I'll be as quick as possible, okay?"

"Go on. You and Ethan go do what you need to do." She smiles, and my heart kicks into overdrive. If she only knew what my errand was.

"Don't answer the door for anyone but me or Ethan, got it?" Her face falls instantly. I'm sure a million questions are running through her mind right now.

"Adam, you're scaring me. Is everything okay?"

No. "Yeah, just something I have to take care of." I kiss her quickly and turn to Ethan. "Ready?"

Thankfully, he doesn't start his inquisition until we are in my truck. "What are we really doing, Adam?" he asks as I back out of my driveway onto the road.

"That call I got. It was Ryder informing me that Riley's bail was posted again…last night." My hands grasp the steering wheel so tight that my knuckles are completely white.

"Shit…"

"I think it's about time I pay him a little visit." I ground my jaw and step on the gas.

"Listen, I know you're pissed off, but you need to be smart. If I remember correctly, you stopped me from beating him to a pulp. Think of Kaylee. Think of the twins. You can't be there to protect them if you're in jail." I know this. I'm not planning to touch him. I just want to…talk…preferably with my fist, but still we are going to have a talk.

"I'm just going to have a little chat." And maybe I might break his neck, his legs, his arms…hell, I want to break every bone in his body, but none of it will compare to the amount of pain Kaylee has suffered because of him.

Ethan lets out a string of curses. "Don't do anything stupid, Adam," he reminds me.

My anger only escalates when I turn down the long, paved driveway to the two-story mansion sitting back on the hill. When I finally reach the house, I throw my truck in park and jump out. Red. That's all I see at this particular second. Ethan is hot on my heels all the way up the sidewalk. My fist connects with the door harshly several times before I finally let my arm drop to my side.

I stand there a good fifteen seconds before the door swings open to reveal just the person I came to see. Before I can contemplate the consequences of my actions, I right hook him, hitting him square in the jaw. Riley stumbles back, but he regains his footing quickly. Ethan instantly locks his arms around me and hauls me back. I'm fuming at the seams. I have never been this pissed off in my entire life.

I thrash around trying to break free of his hold so I can go at him again. "For goodness' sakes, Adam, stop! Think of my sister and how this will affect her! If she knew you were doing this, it would destroy her! You just got her back, man!" I instantly stop fighting and let my arms hang by my sides. "Now…I'm going to let you go and you're going to walk back to your truck and get in the passenger seat, got it?" I let him know I hear him loud and clear. He releases me and I do what he says. I slam the truck door and immediately take out my anger on the dash in front of me. I lean back against the seat and close my eyes. Kaylee is the first thing to pop into my head. Ethan's right; by coming over here, I'm just hurting her more.

Ethan finally gets in the truck looking just as disheveled as I do. "He is a damn good actor, I'll give him that." Before I can ask what he is talking about, he continues. "He claims he wasn't the one who left the note."

"That's bullshit!"

"I know it." We are silent for a couple of miles before Ethan speaks up again. "You look like shit, by the way. Kaylee is going to be pissed." I know this already; he doesn't have to keep reminding me.

"Hey, I need you to swing by the nearest store that has flowers."

Ethan laughs, amused by the fact that I'm only buying the flowers hoping she won't kill me. "As soon as she sees the flowers, she is going to know you did something you shouldn't have. Not to mention you busted your knuckles. Awesome right hook, by the way."

Once we make the pit stop for Kaylee's flowers, we are on our way back home. My stomach is in knots wondering how Kaylee will react. I pray she won't leave me again.

The knots in my stomach tighten when we arrive back at my house. Ethan slaps me on the back. "Well, it's been nice knowing you."

"Shut up," I grumble.

"I'll try and help you out, but if she turns on me, I'm out."

*Thanks…how reassuring.*

I pause at the door and inhale deeply. Might as well get this over with.

*Kaylee*

*"My breath hitches every time Adam walks into the
room. I catch myself gazing at him longing more
often than not." –Kaylee*

I'm sitting on the couch when Adam and Ethan
arrive home looking like they've been in a fight. Adam
more so than Ethan. Adam's knuckles on his right hand are
bleeding a little and he and Ethan both look heated. After
he had warned me not to answer the door for anyone, I
started to worry about where he was going. I trusted that he
would fill me in when he got back or sometime later.

"Oh, my God! Adam, what happened to you?" I run
up to him and start looking for more injuries. He holds up
his left hand that has a bouquet of red roses. When I don't
take the flowers, he lays them down on the end table.

I fold my arms across my chest and shift my weight
to one leg. "Lucas Adam Thomas, what did you do?" My
brother barks out a laugh and says, "I told you, man."
Adam and I level a glare at him, but it is mine that makes
him shut up. Just then, Anna and Alexis enter the living
room. Anna starts worriedly asking the same questions I
have.

"Mom, let me talk to Kaylee first, and then I will
talk to you, all right?" Anna's mouth forms a thin line
before she turns around and walks back to the kitchen. He
holds out his hand and I willingly take it. My mind is
conjuring up all possible scenarios that he will throw my
way as I follow him. When we are in his room, he lets go of
my hand and sits on the bed, burying his head in his hands.

"Adam, you're scaring me," I admit with a shaky voice.

He looks up from the floor and opens his arms for me. I walk into his embrace and wrap my arms around his neck. His head rests against my stomach while my fingers toy with his hair. "I got a call from Ryder," he starts. When he says Ryder, I tense. Adam must have noticed because his hands start moving rhythmically along my back. "His bail was posted last night." He didn't have to say his name because I knew. I start shivering, but not because I am cold. "I wanted to just talk to him, threaten him, hoping he will leave you alone. I had Ethan go with me in case all hell broke loose and thank God, I did. The moment he opened the door…I was so pissed off at everything he has put you through. I got one punch in and your brother stopped me. Ethan wouldn't let me go until I calmed down and got in the truck. I know I shouldn't have gone over there, I'm sorry for that, but all I kept thinking about was how he hurt you and he is getting away with it."

I tilt his face up so I can look in his eyes. Anger is still swimming in his eyes.

"I'm not happy that you went over there, but I forgive you. Just promise me that you will not do anything stupid like that again."

"I swear, sweetheart, I won't do it again." He slowly lifts up my t-shirt, uncovering my belly. He places two kisses on my barely rounded stomach. My heart melts watching him. He then grabs my hand and tugs me forward. I lift one knee up and place it one side of his waist, then I do the same with the other. His arms come around me, holding me tightly against him. He trails feather-like kisses up my neck, along my jaw, and all the way to my slightly parted lips. "I. Love. You. So. Damn. Much," he murmurs between kisses. He trails his hand up my side, cupping the back of my neck. He continues kissing with a passion only found between two people who are right for each other.

Someone knocks on the door, startling us both. I jump out of his lap and run my hands along my shirt, making sure it is smooth and not twisted or anything. I take a couple of deep breaths to try to slow my ragged breathing. The knock sounds again and I realized that neither of us has answered. Adam walks forward, grabs my hand, and smiles warmly at me, bringing my hand up to kiss the back of it. He reaches for the door and I pray that it isn't one of his parents on the other side. When Adam opens the door, revealing Alexis, I release the breath I had been holding. She gives me a knowing smile and a wink causing my face to heat. She knew exactly what was going on in here. "I just came to inform you that lunch is ready."

"We were just on our way out," Adam says coolly.

"Of course, you were," she says, her voice dripping with sarcasm. We follow her down the hall and I pray once more, hoping that no one else can tell what we've been up to.

The food is laid out on the table and everyone is already seated but us. I sit between Alexis and Adam. He moves his hand under the table to rest it on my thigh. Alexis leans in and whispers, "Girl, it's written all over your face." I smack her arm, warning her to quit making me blush.

Anna cooked baked ravioli, green beans, mashed potatoes, and rolls. It all smells wonderful. I hope the little ones like all of this.

Anna gives Adam a stern look. "So Adam, do you want to tell me what is going on?"

Adam clears his throat before speaking. "I think I should start with last night first." I ease my hand under the table and grab his.

Adam dives into the story of what has transpired since I last saw her. Like me, Anna and Jack aren't happy he went over there. He could have gotten himself hurt or worse. We'll be lucky if Riley doesn't turn him in. I'm happy he thought to take Ethan with him. I'm also glad Ethan didn't do anything stupid.

The rest of lunch passes without drama as we sit, talk, and laugh about random things. Time is passing and soon I will have to make a decision about who to stay with. I love it here with Adam and his family, but I miss my brother and I want to spend time with him. Then again, I don't want to miss cuddling with Adam anymore at night. The time we were apart was torture enough. I rely on Adam's help to get through my nightmares, which thankfully, don't come that often anymore. If I'm ever going to get past what Riley has done to me, then maybe I need to face them on my own. My first therapy appointment is in a few days. I'm really nervous about it since I don't like retelling what happened to me. I know it's part of it, but it's painful to get out. Adam will be there with me, and knowing that helps to calm my nerves some. I wouldn't have agreed to it if he hadn't said he would be there with me. Bless his heart; he is trying so hard to help me. The only way I know to repay him is to break free of my demons. I wish this whole thing with Riley was done and over with, and I wish that Mom would just not contact me. I haven't heard from her since the court ruling and seeing her on TV, but I'm not holding my breath. I have a feeling she's not done. Hopefully, she won't find out that I am pregnant. Who knows what she will say or do then?

A little while later, we are camped out in the living room watching some game show. Jack went to his garage to get something and Anna had to run an errand so it's just me, Adam, Ethan, and Alexis. Adam and I are cuddling on the couch. Alexis is sitting next to me, texting Brad I assume, while Ethan is in the recliner in the corner. I figure it's now or never. "Adam, Ethan, can I talk to you?" They both nod as Ethan turns off the TV. I get off the couch and stand. "Okay, I've made a decision on who I want to stay with for now." Both look like they are holding their breath, waiting for my answer. "Adam, I love you, but I need to spend some time with my brother while I'm on break from school. Another reason is that I want to face my nightmares, if I have them, alone. I've thought about it and I've concluded that if I'm ever going to get past this then I have to do this. You're always telling me how strong I am. Well, now I'm going to be."

Adam hugs me tight. "I'm proud of you, sweetheart. You amaze me."

Ethan jumps up from his seat. "Yes! Haha, sucker!" he cheers. I punch his arm in warning, causing him to grunt. "Ouch, sis. You have some bony knuckles."

"You'll do well to remember that, too."

"I'm going to miss you like hell, especially at night," Adam grumbles. I know how he feels. I've debated whether I'm making the right decision because I'm going to miss cuddling with him at night, too.

Alexis snorts, amused with Adam's comment to me. "Oh please, it's not like you won't be over there all the time anyways." In my peripherals, I catch Ethan rolling his eyes.

"Well, baby girl, I need to head on out. Brad is picking me up at seven so I need to start getting ready. Text me later. Love ya!" She hugs me and waves to the guys on her way out the door.

Adam begrudgingly helps me pack some more of my clothes. He told Ethan he would bring me over there in a little while. I think he is putting off me leaving. Anna hugged me so long that I didn't think she'd ever let go.

When we finally reach Ethan's apartment, it is going on eight o'clock. Ethan stopped at the grocery store on the way home and stocked up on food. He even bought my favorite ice cream, which I'm surprised he still remembers.

I walk Adam to the door when he goes to leave. "You know you can call me if you need me. I don't care what it is or what time; call me. You know I'll come running. Make sure you don't answer the door for anyone you don't know and don't stay here alone. If he has to leave, call me." He looks up from me to Ethan. "Make sure she eats properly, gets plenty of rest, and also if she gets sick, I want to know-"

Ethan cuts him off before he adds more to the list. "Dude, I got this. I know how to take care of my sister."

Oh, Adam. He is taking this hard. I frame his face in my hands, forcing him to look at me. "Adam, I'll be fine. I promise to call you if I need you." I reach up and plant a kiss on his lips.

He sighs audibly. "I love you, sweetheart." He kisses me long and hard. Apparently, he took too long, or too long by Ethan's standards, because Ethan clears his throat, breaking us apart.

"Love you, Adam." He gives me his heart-dropping smile one last time before opening the door and leaving.

Ethan claps his hands together and a huge smile appears on his face. "So, sis, what do you want to do first? I've got a ton of movies, a couple of board games, an Xbox, and plenty of junk food."

And so my first night with Ethan begins.

## Ethan

*"There is a girl who plagues my dreams at night. It sucks because I can't have her." –Ethan*

I can't help but sit here and stare at my little sister and think about how much has changed in the last four years. She'll be turning eighteen soon and become a mom in a few months. After everything, she still finds a reason to smile. We are sitting on the floor around the coffee table playing Monopoly. I can't remember the last time we played this together.

I remember the day I got the call from Mom. When I answered the phone, she was crying, and I didn't ever remember a time that she cried. That was just how Mom was, so when I heard her crying, I knew it was bad. I remembered being shocked into silence because Mom had to yell at me to get my attention. Kaylee and I, we have a tight bond that I didn't think would ever be broken. I drove like a madman to the hospital to only find out that my father was dead and my sister didn't want to see me. At first, I didn't believe it. She needed me, right? I was her big brother; she had to need me. She's always needed me. Especially with Dad gone now. Then I thought she was just in shock and needed time to process it all. So I left and came back the next day, figuring I'd given her enough time. Elizabeth stopped me in the hallway again and told me that she didn't want to see me for a while because I reminded her too much of Dad. So I walked away again and forced myself to wait. I waited too long because when I finally got the courage to go to her house, it was empty and I had no idea where they'd moved to. I was so mad and hurt that I trashed my room.

A few months later, I enlisted in the Army and that summer I left for basic training and then AIT training. When I was done with both, I started searching for her. I didn't get to search long because I was sent overseas. Came back nine months later and started searching again. I enlisted the help of a friend of mine, who knew a guy, to help. That's when I found out she was only an hour away from me. I drove there the same day and rode around until I found where she lived. I eventually decided to move to Bowling Green, where Kaylee and her mom were living, after a long discussion with Mom. It's been four years; surely, she would want to see me by now. Really, I just needed answers. I wanted to know why she shut me out and why she couldn't tell me to my face that she didn't want to see me. Plus, Dad made me promise before he died that when he passed on, I'd give Kaylee a letter. I made that promise the day he told me he had cancer and was dying. I held it in when I was in front of him, but as soon as I was in my car, it all came out. I remembered asking him a ton of questions. Was the cancer treatable? Had he told Kaylee? When he answered no to telling Kaylee, I asked him why. Not even a month later, I got the call from Mom.

The first time I saw her in four years, I found my sister at Dad's grave. She was sitting on the ground in front of the marble tombstone talking to him. I wanted to go up to her and get her to talk to me, but I decided I needed to wait until she was done spending time with Dad. Out of the corner of my eye, I noticed her friends off to the side, glaring at me. They obviously didn't know who I was or why I was watching Kaylee. At least they were protective of her. I felt better knowing that. The guy, who I was hoping was just a friend, walked up to Kaylee and wrapped his arm around her. I wanted to walk up and rip his arm off her, but I changed my mind and walked away. Today was not the day to talk to her. Not while she was mourning.

After that day, it seemed like I couldn't find her. Every time I went to her house, she was not there. I realized she had school, but I figured she would be home by six? I was trying to time it when Kaylee's mom, Elizabeth, wasn't there. I couldn't stand the woman. The feeling was mutual with her, as well. No doubt she'd slam the door in my face.

When someone finally answered the door, it wasn't my sister; it was her friend. Her beauty floored me. For a moment, I forgot where I was and why I was there. I finally cleared my throat and willed my voice to work. "Is Kaylee here?"

She gives me a wary look. "She doesn't live here."

Why was she lying to me? Did Kaylee know I'd been looking for her? Was that why her friend answered the door? "Yes, she does. I know for a fact she does."

She assessed me, looking me up and down. I cleared my throat once more, trying to get her back to the conversation at hand. Her eyes shot up to mine and she held her finger up. "One second." She closed the door, leaving me wondering what she was doing. Was she talking to Kaylee? If so, what was Kaylee saying? When the door reopened, the same girl was there. I took in her stature, noticing her squared shoulders. She was noticeably standing taller. "You need to leave. If you don't, I'll be forced to call the cops."

"Fine." I'd play. *One day, Kaylee. We will talk.*

Once again, every time I would go back to the house, no one would be there or answer the door. I knew they hadn't moved again because the house was still furnished. One night, I even parked my truck across the street just to see if Kaylee ever came home. She didn't. Which begged the question, "Where was she?"

A month later and still no luck. Every now and then, I would still park my truck across where she lived and wait for her to come home, but she never did.

I stopped for lunch one day at a restaurant, needing to come up with another plan; not to mention I was going to need to get a job soon. I wanted to apply for a position at the local police department since it would go along with my military training. Eventually, I wanted to work my way up to detective and work with homicides. I wanted to help bring justice to families whose loved ones were stolen from them, like mine.

I didn't know if it was sheer luck or coincidence when I saw Kaylee walk into Machino's. She was with the same guy who was at the cemetery. I was now thinking they were dating. My hands fist together when I noticed his arm around her. Then I noticed the brace that was covering practically her whole leg. What happened there? She didn't notice me at all. When she sat down, her back was to me. The guy she was with stole a chair from another table so she could prop her leg up. I was glaring heatedly at him now. They were talking, but I was too far back to hear what their conversation was about. Judging by him grabbing her hand and…kissing it, it seemed that he was reassuring her about something. I leaned back in my chair and just watched them. When his gaze traveled over her shoulder and met mine, his eyes flared in recognition. We glared at each other, neither one of us breaking our hard stares until Kaylee got his attention. When he returned to look at me again, I matched his look with one of my own. We stayed like that until Kaylee turned to see who he was looking at. Her eyes widened when she saw me and she quickly spun back around. I signaled for the waitress and paid the check. Once she returned with my change, I threw some bills on the table for a tip and stand. It was time this shit got settled. I wouldn't let her get away without answering my questions. Her boyfriend saw me coming and automatically stood. I was shocked when he got between us and smarted off to me.

I turned into a raging bull when I learned they were living together. There was no reason she should be shacking up with a guy. It answered why she was never home, though. My eyes averted to her left hand for a ring. Thank God, there was not one. I'd really blow a fuse then.

I follow them to "their" house, feeling a little unsure of how this is going to go. Kaylee doesn't seem to want to talk to me still. My heart aches for the bond we had. I want us to put all of this behind us and be close again.

Since that day, we have been slowly rebuilding our relationship. Kaylee was once outgoing, never shy. She was not at all afraid to ask you a question. Now, life has her hiding, scared to be the girl she was once was.

Kaylee narrows her blue eyes at me when she notices me assessing her. "What? Do I have something on my face?" Her hands automatically fly up to her face.

I laugh it off and shake my head. Inside, my gut is twisting at the uneasy feeling I get when I think about how much has changed. I think back to when Adam mentioned how strong she is. Kaylee is becoming one of the strongest people I know. I see the strength before me now. Even when she looks broken, I see a glimpse of it. She makes me so proud. Growing up, I taught her to be strong, to stand up for herself, and not to let anyone steal her happiness. I knew I wouldn't always be around so I wanted her to be able to care for herself if need be. Other than strength, happiness is still there. I don't foresee it going away, either.

While she is staying with me, I want to instill those principals in her again. I don't want her to be the little thirteen-year-old sister I once knew, I want her to be who she wants to be. She wants to beat the demons that are plaguing her and I'm willing give her a little nudge of confidence to help. I have a few ideas of my own that might help.

*"I'm pretty sure not having her constantly around
me the next two weeks is going to slowly kill me."
–Adam*

Ethan and I have been sitting around the apartment
all morning, but now it's time for me to get ready for my
first therapy appointment. Adam will be here in forty-five
minutes, and I have yet to get in the shower. I'm
procrastinating is what I'm doing. I dread this because I'm
not ready to face my feelings. I need to do this even though
I don't want to. Yes, it will bring back unwanted memories.
Yes, it will be painful. I will never be truly ready to try and
get past what happened four years ago. But for Adam, I
will try. He makes me want to face my demons and defeat
them. I finally made myself head for the shower, cursing
myself because now I will have to rush through it.

I'm out of the shower and drying off twenty
minutes later. I throw my clothes on and brush out my hair.
I don't even bother to style my hair or put on make-up.
Why would I when it will just be messed up in a bit? I did,
however, put on jeans instead of sweatpants like I wanted
to. Unfortunately, by wearing jeans, I learn that pretty soon
I'm going to need bigger ones.

Ethan is stretched out on the recliner watching TV
when I walk in. I decide to sit on the couch and wait until
Adam arrives. Ethan looks up from the TV over to me. "I
fixed you some tomato soup. It's sitting in the microwave."

Tomato soup sounds pretty good right now. "Thank
you," I say when I walk past him. I grab the soup and pour
myself something to drink before heading back to the

couch. I'm pretty sure I have ten minutes or so before Adam gets here. I was hoping I wouldn't have to scarf down the soup.

"Have I ever met your mom?" I ask Ethan out of nowhere.

"No, you haven't, at least not to my knowledge. Elizabeth wouldn't allow it, I don't think."

"What's that supposed to mean?"

Ethan sits up in the recliner, resting his arms on his knees. I can tell he isn't sure how to answer my question. "I don't know the whole story, but I think it's because Elizabeth's jealous of my mom."

"What is she like?" She has to be better than mine. When a smile forms on his face, he proves it.

"She's wonderful, she's polite, and she's always the peacemaker. She's beautiful inside and out. I couldn't ask for a better mother." Why couldn't my mother be like that? Why was I stuck with one who never appreciated me?

"I know what you're thinking, Kaylee. I wish Elizabeth would actually be a mother, but we have to accept reality and move on."

I nod and continue eating the last few spoonsful of my soup. "Did your mom ever remarry?"

Ethan shakes his head. "She has dated a couple of men, but nothing has ever come out of it. I honestly think she's happy with her life the way it is."

"I'm happy for her." Ethan smiles warmly at my honesty.

A knock on the front door causes me to jump. Ethan gets up and walks to the door. It's been a little over a week since the letter was left for me and I still jump at sudden noises. Nothing has happened since. No more notes, no nothing, but I still look over my shoulder at times, as if I can feel someone watching me. Maybe…hopefully, I'm just paranoid.

Ethan checks the peephole before opening it and letting Adam inside. I leap off the couch and into his arms. I haven't seen him much in the last few days. Needless to say, I've missed him.

"You need to relax, sweetheart," he murmurs in my ear.

"I'm fine, Adam." Now that I have my arms around him.

"You're tense." I exhale and force my body to relax. "That's better. Are you ready to go?"

"As ready as I'll ever be." I break our hug and pick up my wristlet and keys off the couch. I say good-bye to Ethan and put on my jacket. I sigh inwardly and grab Adam's hand. *Let's get this over with.*

I gaze out the window of Adam's truck at the building to our right. I take a deep breath and release it. Sitting here, right now, I wish I wasn't doing this. It's so nerve-wracking.

The truck door opens as Adam steps in my line of vision. My eyes automatically fix on him. He stretches his hand out to me, and I willingly take it. Once he helps me out of the truck, he wraps his arm around my waist. I take the opportunity to embrace him. I lean my head against his chest and his arms enclose around me. He sighs and kisses my hair before letting his mouth fall to mine. "Remember, sweetheart, I've got you." I know he does. He had me on my first day back to school.

The words were lodged in my throat so I just nod. He pulls away and grabs my hand, leading me toward the building. I am so nervous that I'm shaking.

We walk in and give the receptionist our names. She instructs us to take a seat, and that it will be just a moment. I'm so glad Adam is with me. I wouldn't have made it to the parking lot before I chickened out and went home.

We wait ten minutes then our names are called. I squeeze Adam's hand as we walk into Dr. Lawson's office. Her office has an "earthy" feel to it. Everything in her office is in either brown, green, or yellow. We take a seat on the medium brown loveseat in the middle of the room. We shake hands with Dr. Lawson and introduce ourselves.

"Before we start, I'd like to inform you that anything you tell me is strictly confidential. Nothing you say in here will leave this room. Any questions before we begin?" When Adam and I both shake our heads, she continues. "If at any time you think of a question, please don't hesitate to ask. Now, what can I do you?"

Adam clears his throat. "Kaylee has been through some pretty tough situations and I thought coming here would help her. I'm just here for support."

"Are you two a couple?"

"Yes," Adam answers instantly.

"How about we start from the beginning. Kaylee, tell me, what do you want to talk about first?"

I swallow past the lump in my throat. "My father was murdered in front of me four years ago."

"I'm sorry to hear that. How old were you at the time?"

"Thirteen." I watch as she scribbles on her notepad. I wonder what she's writing.

"Do you feel responsible for his death?"

I squeeze Adam's hand. "Yes."

"Why? What transpired that day that led you to believe such a thing?"

I swallow hard, fighting back the tears that burn my eyes. Adam squeezes my hand encouragingly. As I tell her, I keep my eyes downcast. I stare at our joined hands as I force the words out. I have to stop a couple of times to compose myself, but thankfully, I make it through the story. It is as painful and heartbreaking as I thought it would be.

"How many times have you talked with someone about it?"

"My best friend knows a little, but other than her, just Adam."

"And what did they say?"

"They said it wasn't my fault."

"They're right, Kaylee. You're a survivor. Tell me, has anyone been charged for the crime?"

"No, they closed the case because they had no leads."

"I think maybe you feel responsible for what happened to you and your father because the men were never arrested and charged for a crime they committed. Am I right?" Is she right? I've never thought about it like that.

I shrug one shoulder. "Maybe...I don't know. I haven't thought about it."

"Why do you feel that it's your fault?"

"Because I kept bugging him. If I had just left it alone and waited until the next day as he suggested in the first place..." I trail off not wanting to finish the sentence.

"Has anyone told you that it was your fault?"

"Yes," I whisper. "My mom blames me."

"How was your relationship with your mother before? Did you get along well?"

"We weren't close, but we got along. She never seemed mad or upset with me until recently. I always wondered if she did, deep down, blame me. I guess I know now." Hearing Mom say that she has always blamed me was a punch to the gut.

"How often do you and your mother talk?"

"Not often."

"When was the last time you talked to her?"

"A week ago when we went to court." Dr. Lawson eyes me curiously so I go ahead and explain. "I'm emancipated from her now. She said some pretty awful things to me after…" I didn't want to say what happened to me aloud. It's embarrassing and it hurts too much to think about, let alone talk.

"After…" she presses. Dang it, I knew she wouldn't drop it. "Is this something different that happened or are you still talking about your father?"

The lump in my throat grows. I wipe my free hand on my jeans. My other hand has a death grip on Adam's. "Something different," I murmur. "Can we not talk about it today, though?" I think I've had enough for one day.

"Sure but at some point you will need to talk about it, Kaylee. I know it's hard to talk about things that have happened to us, but I promise you, talking helps." She pauses a moment before turning her attention to Adam. "Is there anything you would like to talk about or say to Kaylee?"

Adam clears his throat and shifts so he is facing me. I know Adam, so whatever he is going to say will more than likely make me cry. "I want you to know how proud I am of you for doing this. It takes a lot of courage. I know I have told you this several times already, but you are so strong. You never give up after being knocked down. You're doing great, sweetheart. I love you."

With my eyes full of tears, I reply, "I love you, too."

"What a good way to end our first session. If you two don't have any questions, I'll see you in two weeks." We thank her and say good-bye.

I feel relief when I step out of the office. The first session felt brutal to me. I know one session doesn't cure me, but I thought I would at least feel a little lighter. The highlight of the session was Adam telling me how proud he is. Opening up to people is not for me. I hate spilling out my feelings to someone I don't know.

"What do you think?" Adam asks once we settle back in his truck.

"It was uncomfortable talking about those things. I know that is part of it, but…it's…it's just so hard." He clasps my hand, bringing it to his mouth, and kisses it.

"I know, sweetheart, but keeping it all in isn't healthy and only hurts you more. Why don't we attend two more sessions, and after that, if you still don't think it's helping, we won't go anymore?"

"Okay, I'll keep trying. Thank you for sticking by me. I couldn't do this without you."

"I wouldn't want to be anywhere else." I wouldn't want him to, either.

## 7

*Ethan*

*"I'm going to prove to him I'm who he wants. I'm going to bring his hidden feelings to the surface so even he can't deny it." –Alexis*

Kaylee just asked me if her best friend, Alexis, could come over. First of all, I don't understand why she feels she has to ask for permission. Secondly, I can't decide if I want her friend to come. On one hand, she's smoking hot. On the other, she's my little sister's best friend...and seventeen.

Alexis.

How can I describe her without sounding so...hypnotized? Her five-foot-six frame stands just three inches shorter than I do. Her jet-black hair makes her emerald eyes shine. Her slim body would fit perfectly under mine. Shit, I need to quit thinking of her like that. It can't happen; she's too young. I can go to jail for that shit.

"Ethan!" Kaylee shouts my name, pulling me from my forbidden thoughts. "Are you okay?" she asks, her voice full of concern.

No. Not really. "Of course! Why?" I say with a little too much enthusiasm.

She eyes me suspiciously. "You were staring into space like you were looking at something dreamy." Shit.

How am I going to explain that? "Uh, are you sure?" Maybe I can make her believe she was seeing things.

"Um, yeah, I'm positive. Your face was all like..." Kaylee then tries to recreate the face I was supposedly making. My sister, everyone.

"I seriously doubt I made that face." I'm sure I did, but I can't come up with an excuse as to why I made said face. I grab the decorative pillow that my mom thought I needed and chunk it at Kaylee. She catches it easily and sets it down in her lap.

"You never answered me, you know."

"Answered what?"

Her palm smacks her forehead. "Such a guy," she mumbles out loud. "I asked you if you cared if Alexis came over for a while." Oh, right…I knew that.

Alexis. Damn…even her name is a turn on.

A pillow hits me upside my head, snapping me back to reality. "There you go with that dreamy look again. Spill, brother."

"I have no idea what you're talking about, sis."

"Whatever. Don't think I don't know who you're thinking about when you get that look." She crosses her arms like she is calling out my shit.

"And who would I be thinking about?"

"Don't play dumb, Ethan. I know you like Alexis. Every time I say her name, you get that same look on your face."

"Do not," I argue.

'Do too," she fires back.

"Do not."

Kaylee throws her hands in the air. "Ugh! You're so annoying! Why can't you just admit it! And you still never answered my question!"

I pinch the bridge of my nose. "Kaylee, for the love of God, you don't have to ask for permission! This is your apartment, too!"

"Why are you so irritated?"

"Why do you ask so many questions? Seriously, how does Adam put up with you?"

"And you say I'm the one asking too many questions," she mutters under her breath.

Ignoring her, I pull out my phone to check the time. "Get up sis, we've got to go or we're going to be late."

"What time do you think we'll be back? Six or seven?"

"Somewhere around there." Kaylee types back a reply to Alexis, I assume, then deposits her phone in her back pocket.

We weren't twenty minutes down the road, and Kaylee's eyes started drooping. A minute later, she's out cold. I turn on the radio and find a station to listen to, hoping the rest of the drive passes quickly.

I'm about ten minutes away from Mom's when my phone rings so I pick it up out of the console. Adam's name flashes on the screen. "Yeah," I say when I answer.

"Kaylee's with you, right?" he asks sounding panicked.

"Of course, she's with me. We are on our way to visit my mom. Where did you think she was?"

I hear him exhale. "Why isn't she answering her phone? I've called her like fifty times."

"Maybe because she's asleep."

"Why is she asleep? Is she feeling all right?" Now he is in panic mode again.

"Dude, chill, she's fine. She's been aggravating me all morning; trust me when I say she's fine." That makes him laugh. "No offense, and I even asked her this, but how do you put up with her? She's my sister and I love her to death, but seriously does she not make you want to pull your hair out?"

"No, not really. I think it's just you. You can always send her back anytime, ya know." Like hell, she may annoy the crap out of me, but that doesn't mean I'm going to boot her out of my apartment.

"She's not annoying me that much."

"Damn, it was worth a shot."

"I'm sure you'll get her back soon enough. Let me enjoy my time with her while I have her." I quickly glance at Kaylee, who is still asleep. She is curled up in the seat with her head resting on the center console.

"I get it, man. Tell her to call me later." I assure him that I will and hang up. It takes me a couple of minutes to wake up Kaylee, but she is finally awake and sitting up when I pull into Mom's gravel drive.

"Ready?" Kaylee looks like she is about to puke. "Don't worry, sis. Mom is really excited to meet you."

She looks at me with hope in her eyes. "Are you serious? She really wants to meet me?" The underlying question is, "She doesn't hate me?"

"You have no idea. When I asked her if we could come visit her, she screamed in my ear. I swear I thought she had busted my eardrum. That's how excited she is, so be prepared." I could barely hear out of my right ear for an hour. Mom has been waiting for the day she got to meet her.

I climb out of my truck and wait for her to walk around the front of the truck. When she is next to me, we start walking along the sidewalk that leads to the front door.

"Wait," Kaylee suddenly says as he grabs my arm, pulling me a halt. "How much does she know about me?"

"She knows everything." The day I found out everything, I was so upset I called Mom and revealed what I had learned the first day I talked to her. A lot of hate and angry words were used in the conversation. "I hope you don't mind," I add quickly.

"No, it's cool. It saves me from having to do it." I nod and we continue up the sidewalk.

As we hit the first step, the front door swings open and Mom comes bursting through. "Oh my, I can't believe it! You're finally here!" Mom runs straight to Kaylee and pretty much tackles her. "You're as beautiful as I thought you'd be!" Mom is still squeezing Kaylee to death while gushing over her.

"Mom, let her breathe a little," I say as I try to pry Mom off Kaylee. Mom releases her and grabs her hand, pulling her to the house. "Told you so," I say so only Kaylee can hear.

*Kaylee*

Ethan asks his mom and me if we want anything. I ask for a water and he nods and leaves for the kitchen. When he returns, we are sitting in the den. He hands me the water and I thank him.

"Oh dear, I'm glad you're here! You don't know how long I've been waiting for this day."

"I'm glad that I get to meet you as well. I have a few questions that I'd like to ask you if that's okay. If it's too personal, you don't have to answer." I don't want her to think I'm nosy or something.

"Honey, you can ask me anything. What do you want to know?"

"Why did you and my father split? Did you still talk afterward?"

A small laugh escapes her. "Honestly, we were more friends than we were lovers. That's how we started out, as friends. Then we decided to try dating. We dated for about a year and then we, on a whim, got married. Our parents were so mad at us for having a 'shotgun' wedding, as they called it. Everyone thought the reason for our marriage was that I was pregnant. At first, I laughed and told them they were crazy, but two weeks later, I found out that I actually was. One day, your father and I were talking and we concluded that we weren't as in love as we thought. So, we decided to part ways and remain friends before our friendship was severed. We talked regularly after the divorce, even when he started to date Elizabeth. I never really liked her, and I was honest with him about it. Boy, was he wrapped around her finger. She had him convinced that I was jealous. We didn't talk much after that. I believe she gave him an ultimatum, and he chose her.

"When I got the news that she was pregnant, my first thought was, 'Lord, please do not let that child turn out like her mother.' He must've listened because your personality is just like your father's."

Why couldn't Julie and Dad have stayed together and had one more kid? I still would've turned out good because both Julie and Dad have kind personalities.

"Why wasn't I allowed to come visit you?"

Julie pats my hand and sighs. "Your father thought it was a wonderful idea, but sadly, your mother didn't. She didn't want him to have anything to do with me. There were times when she tried to convince your dad not to meet me so he could get Ethan. There was no way I would give my child to her and there was no way your father would miss time with Ethan. That's what I loved about Jason the most, how devoted he was." I can definitely say that about Dad, too. He was at every game, every recital. Anywhere I needed him, he was there.

"You don't blame me for what happened to Dad, do you?" I don't feel like she does, but my insecurities are running wild.

She leans over and pulls me in for a hug. "No honey, I don't and you shouldn't either. Ethan's told me everything that is going on and words can't express how sorry I am that you're going through this. I know it's a rough time for you and if you ever need me, you can always call me."

I pull away and thank her. "I think that's all the questions I have."

"Okay dear, but if you ever think of any, I'll be happy to answer them the best I can."

We spend the rest of the afternoon sharing stories of my dad and getting pregnancy advice. I was nervous about even coming because I didn't know what to expect, but I'm glad I came. It is going on five thirty by the time we go to leave. I wave good-bye and tell her that I'll visit again soon.

Once we are in Ethan's truck, I pull out my phone and send a quick text to Alexis letting her know that we are on our way home and that she can just meet me at Ethan's apartment in an hour. I notice Adam called several times, too.

"I want to make a detour right quick. There is something I want to show you," Ethan announces out of the blue.

Ethan drives into town and turns into the parking lot of a storage business. Once he puts in his passcode, the gate opens and he drives through. He pulls up by one of the lockers and parks his truck. This looks bigger than most of the other ones. I wonder idly what's inside. I imagine I'm about to find out. Ethan unlocks the door and opens it. I stare, open-mouthed at the car sitting in the building.

"What do you think, sis?"

"It's beautiful! What kind of car is it?" I walk inside and admire the car. I want to run my hand along it, but I'm afraid to touch it.

"It's a 1968 Dodge Charger R/T."

"Why is it in here? I would be driving it!" This car is so beautiful. It's a little dusty, but with a good wash, it will be shining. The interior is a mixture of red and black, mostly red with black exterior paint.

"I'm in the process of restoring it. Right now, I'm in the middle of rebuilding the engine. It's going to have a Chrysler 426 Hemi engine when it's all said and done. Within the next week, I'm getting it moved closer to my apartment."

"Why don't you keep it at Dan's shop and just work on it there?" I guess I should talk to Adam and his dad first, but I don't see it being a problem.

"Hmm, I guess I could. I'll run it by Adam and his dad first. Speaking of, you need to call Adam back before he has another panic attack." Panic attack? I look at him like, "What in the world are you talking about?" "He called earlier when you were asleep. He couldn't get you on your phone so he called mine in a panic thinking something happened to you. I told him I'd have you call him later. Oh, and when I told him you were asleep, he started freaking out again thinking you were sick or something."

I smack his arm. "Why didn't you wake me up?"

"Because you obviously were tired and I didn't want a black eye for waking you up."

"When have I ever given you a black eye for waking me up?"

"Summer of 2003. I stayed the weekend and you were still asleep at ten in the morning. I was bored so I went to wake you up. I shook you once and you clocked me." Whoops. "That same summer, two weeks later. Same situation, same outcome."

"I guess you should have learned your lesson the first time," I smirk.

He gives me a pointed look. "Trust me, since that day, I've told myself I wouldn't wake you up ever again. I didn't care if there was a bomb in the house; I wasn't going to be the one to wake you up."

"Seriously? I couldn't have hurt you that bad."

He crosses his arms over his chest, not amused. "I had a black eye for a week. I had to tell my friends that some guy sucker punched me."

I throw my head back and laugh. "Surely, they didn't buy that lame excuse."

He grunts. "Of course, they didn't, and they tortured me with it for the longest time after I told them what really happened."

"Serves you right." He ignores my comment and walks out of the unit. "Little sister beat up big bad brother," I taunt as I follow him out.

"Keep on, Kaylee. Just remember, paybacks are a bitch with a capital B."

"Bring it on, bubba," I challenge him.

## Alexis

*"This so wrong, but then again, it feels so right. I just wish he would notice it, too."- Alexis*

My stomach is a bundle of nerves as I climb out of the shower. I am getting ready to spend time with Kaylee tonight at Ethan's apartment. Excitement bubbles up from underneath the butterflies that decided to make a home in my body. I become a blubbering mess if he is in the same room with me. I try to ignore the looks he gives me so no one can see how bad he has me wound up in knots. When he gazes at me, I squirm in my seat, hoping no one but he notices. I want him to notice how he affects me. I want him to know I want him. I may hide it from everyone else, but I won't hide from him. He seems reserved sometimes, like a closed book. He is going through a lot right now so that may be why he seems closed off.

His striking blue eyes have pierced mine more than once. The way he looks at me has my body buzzing for him. His dark hair is short on the sides and thicker on the top. My fingers itch to twirl the short tendrils around my finger. His square jaw is chiseled to perfection. A light stubble graces it and I want to brush my cheek against it. He's awakening all these feelings inside me by just fixing his eyes on me. Even when he looks at me briefly, I want to jump in his arms and kiss the living hell out of him. I wonder what he would say, how he would respond if I did? Would he kiss me back or turn me down? I would be hurt if he turned me down, but it doesn't mean I would stop trying. I see the lust in his eyes when he gazes impassively at me.

I step into a pair of Miss Me jeans and slip on my hot pink sweater. I make sure to wear my favorite black, lacy push-up bra and matching panty set. I curl my long hair, letting it drape over my shoulders. I apply a little foundation and some eye shadow to help make my eyes pop. My eyelashes are thick and long so I don't have to worry about applying mascara. I gaze at myself in the mirror, making sure everything looks satisfactory. It took me longer to pick out my outfit tonight, so I'm a little later than planned.

My phone chimes, signaling I have a message. It is Kaylee letting me know they are swinging by the apartment to pick me up so I don't go out alone. I want to just get in my car and drive myself over there. I think the guys are overreacting with me.

My phone rings and this time it is Brad. Brad is a charismatic guy; he is respectful, and he is also funny, but I don't think he is the one for me. When we kiss, the spark between us is lacking. Don't get me wrong, he can kiss the hell out of you. I'm just not feeling it.

I swipe my finger across the screen of my phone to answer his call. "Hey," I say sweetly.

"Hey babe, you haven't left yet, have you?"

"No, Kaylee just text me and said they were going to swing by and pick me up."

"Oh." I can tell by his tone that he doesn't like the idea of Ethan coming to get me. Brad is jealous where Ethan is concerned. *He has every right to be.* "I can come pick you up later if you want?"

Is that a good idea? "I'll text you later."

"Okay, just let me know."

"I will." We say good-bye and hang up just as the doorbell rings.

My breathing involuntarily picks up knowing that Ethan is the one on the other side of the door waiting for me. I primp in the mirror one last time, making sure everything is in place. I grab my things off the bed and walk swiftly to the front door. I stop and take a huge breath before turning the knob and opening the door. I suck in a harsh breath when I see him standing there. He is wearing a plain black t-shirt that fits snugly around his arms. It's a wonder the shirt hasn't ripped yet. His dark wash jeans hug him in all the right places. He is mouthwatering hot, as usual.

"You ready?" I just nod because I'm not positive that my voice will work. "Well, let's go then." He steps back, allowing me to walk in front of him. I may have added a little sway to my hips, knowing that he is more than likely staring at my ass.

The moment I hop in the truck, I know he saw my little hip action because, when my eyes meet his in the rearview mirror, they have darkened. On the inside, I am doing a happy dance, but on the outside, my face remains impassive. I really want to smirk at him, letting him know I have him right where I want him. I hope all my flirting will break his resolve. I don't know why he is holding back. I wish he wouldn't.

Kaylee and I chat on the way to the apartment, catching up on things. Ethan just sits quietly, listening to us talk. Occasionally, I'll glance in the rearview mirror and find him looking at me. As soon as he notices me looking, he quickly averts his eyes.

As soon as we walk into the apartment, Kaylee heads straight for the bathroom, leaving me alone with him. I make my way to the kitchen, hunting for something to drink. My hand was just about to grab the handle on the fridge when I'm spun around, coming face to face with Ethan.

"What do you think you're doing, Lex?" he growls, backing me up against the refrigerator. His hands are on either side of my head against the stainless steel. My breathing spikes up the closer he gets. My heart is practically beating out of my chest.

"Exactly what you want me to." His eyes drop to my mouth then back up to my eyes. *Kiss me!*

He sighs and closes his eyes for a brief second then reopens them. "I can't for more than one reason."

"Why?"

"For starters, you are jail bait for a guy like me." Oh, right, our age difference.

I am about to tell him that I'll be eighteen soon when Kaylee hollers, "Hey guys, where'd you go?"

Ethan jumps back hastily and walks away, leaving me panting for him.

Kaylee walks in the kitchen and looks back and forth between us. I'm still in the same spot against the fridge while Ethan has moved over to the sink, hunched over with his hands grasping the countertop, his back to us. She gives me the "we will talk later" look. I just want to know the other reasons why Ethan and I can't be together.

I finally turn and get a Dr. Pepper out of the fridge.

I hear Ethan clear his throat. "If you girls are hungry, I can order a pizza."

"Thank goodness, 'cause I'm starving!" Kaylee bellows.

Ethan laughs at his sister. "You're always hungry, preggo."

"That's because I have two reasons why."

I love the banter between them. I wish he could talk to me as easily as he does her.

"True. What kind of pizza do you want?" For the first time since Kaylee has walked in, he finally looks at me. It is brief, but I will take all the gazes from him I can get.

Kaylee and I decide on a pepperoni pizza. While Ethan orders, we venture into the living room to pick out a movie. It takes us several minutes to settle on a movie since practically all of his are action or horror. We finally browse through Netflix and find something we both like. We grab several blankets and pillows from the closet and the beds to create a pallet on the floor.

Kaylee and I stifle our laughs when we hear Ethan groan. "Seriously?! Did you two have to pick a chick flick?"

We just roll our eyes and get comfortable on our pallet before we start *The Notebook*.

Fifteen minutes in, the pizza arrives. Ethan ended up ordering two pizzas, which was a good thing considering Kaylee and I devour a whole one ourselves.

There is a knock on the door halfway into the movie. All three of us look at one another wondering who it could be. Ethan casually stands and walks to the door. Kaylee is clutching my arm to the point it's starting to go numb. The threat has her on edge constantly. I can't say that I blame her. I'd be acting the same if I had a threat directed at me.

I see Ethan relax when he opens the door, but he is blocking my view of who is on the other side. I freeze when I hear a female voice.

"E, why haven't you called me?" the girl whines. Kaylee and I make a gagging sound. Ethan turns around to glare at us, giving me a chance to see what the whiny girl looks like. She is average height and has strawberry blond hair and green eyes. She is wearing a halter-top that displays her breasts and a black leather mini skirt. Her five-inch stilettos put her at almost matching height with Ethan. I want to barf just looking at her. I watch as she turns his attention back to her with her perfectly manicured finger. He steps outside and closes the door behind him.

Kaylee and I waste no time getting up and pressing our ears to the door, wanting to hear their conversation.

*"Who are they?"* the girl whose face I want to bust in asks.

*"My sister and her friend."*

*"Why are they here?"* she asks in disgust.

*"I told you, my sister needed a place to crash for a while. Her friend is just here visiting."*

I hate hearing him call me 'her friend.'

*"Can't they leave for a while?"* Are you kidding me right now?

*"No, they can't. I'll call you tomorrow. Will you be home?"* I really don't want to be listening to this, but I can't pull myself away from the door. This is another reason why he says "he can't" be with me. I hate her right now. What are they? Are they dating? Do they just sleep together? Friends with benefits? Suddenly, I want to know more about their relationship.

*"For you, always. I'll be waiting for your call,"* she says seductively.

We hear the click of her heels and rush back to our spots. We had just fixed the covers when Ethan walked in the door.

"Eavesdropping, girls? Really?"

Kaylee and I smile innocently. "I have no clue what you're talking about, big brother."

"We would never do such a thing," I add, feigning innocence. Inside my chest, the seams of my perfectly sewn heart are unraveling. I shouldn't feel this way while I'm with Brad, yet when I am around Ethan, I have no control over my body and its reaction to him.

My plan to talk to Brad is now being put on hold. Maybe I should actually try to have a relationship with Brad and see where it goes. If one thing's for certain, Brad won't stomp on my heart like Ethan is doing now. Maybe Brad is who I need.

Brad deserves someone better than a girl who is pining over her best friend's brother. I need to stay away from Ethan and his force field that I always seem to walk into. I need to quit thinking of how he makes my heart race and how I can only think of him and his handsome face.

# 9

## Kaylee

*"Watching her and Adam together kills me because I know I screwed up and lost the best thing I could ever have." –Riley*

I grab the nearest pillow next to me and cover my head with it. It's way too early for yelling. Who in their right minds are arguing at this ungodly hour? I groan loudly, letting them know I can hear them loud and clear.

"I can't believe you did that, you asshole!" Alexis screeches, causing me to cringe. I'm going to have a headache if they keep this up.

"I thought I was doing you a favor! Excuse me for trying to help!" Ethan replies, sounding exasperated.

Deciding I've heard enough yelling for one morning, I remove the pillow and sit up. "What in the world are you two fighting about?"

My hands fly to my ears to block out the round of yelling I commenced. They are both trying to tell me what is going on in their own words, at the same time, really loudly. "Hey!" They both grow silent and stare at me. "Now, Alexis, can you please enlighten me as to why you guys are having a screaming match this early in the morning?"

"First of all, Kaylee, it's ten in the morning," she points out. No way, it seems way earlier than that. "Secondly, your asshole of a brother took my phone while I was asleep and sent a text to my mother and Brad telling them I was staying the night here," she huffs and folds her arms across her chest. My fingers massage my temples in an attempt to try to process the mile long sentence she just told me.

I look at my brother who seems equally mad. These two need to get a grip. "Ethan, is that true?"

"Yep," he answers, not denying her accusations. "I thought I was being a gentleman by letting her sleep."

Alexis starts in on him again, and I have to yell to gain her attention. I don't understand why she is flipping out as bad as she is. I think a lot of her anger is stemming from that chick who showed up last night.

"Ethan, apologize, please."

"Hell, no! I did her a favor!"

Crap, now he has awakened the beast. "Oh, please! You didn't do me any favors! My boyfriend was supposed to come pick me up last night because we had plans in the works. Thanks for screwing that up!" Ethan's jaw flexes when she says 'boyfriend.'

"Oh my God, woman! Your phone was blowing up!"

"You should have woke me up!" Alexis jabs her finger in his chest as she yells at him.

I've had enough. "Guys! Please, stop arguing!" Alexis huffs, spinning on her heels and marching into my room. "You two, I swear, are giving me a migraine."

"It's her fault," Ethan grumbles.

"Both of you need to apologize to each other." He starts to argue, but I hold my hand up to stop him. "You shouldn't have messed with her phone."

"I'm not apologizing until she does."

"Whatever." I throw my hands up in defeat. "I'm going to fix myself some breakfast."

I'm sitting at the kitchen table when Alexis walks in. I haven't seen Ethan since I told him I was going to eat. I'm sure he is in his room or something.

"Brad will be here shortly to pick me up," she announces.

"Did you tell him?"

"Yeah, he is pissed."

"I'm sure." I sigh, hoping a fight doesn't break out between them two. I want to question her about what I walked in on last night, but I decide to wait in case Ethan is around the corner, listening.

I say good-bye to Alexis, who is dragging Brad away. He wants to confront Ethan and we won't let him. I hope he is not mad at her for something my brother did.

I grab my clothes for a shower and turn on the water. Adam will be here soon to pick me up. I'm not sure what we are doing today, although I know I'll be happy with whatever since it's with Adam. I miss being with him all day, but I needed to do this for us. I've had a few nightmares and Ethan has comforted me through them. A couple of them were different than my normal ones. The note has spooked me. I want them to be slim to none before I move back in with Adam. I haven't even told him about the new ones yet. I'm afraid to because I know it will just make him worry more and I don't want to add to the stress.

I just finish brushing my teeth when I hear Ethan talking to someone. I assume it's Adam since he is the only visitor we are expecting and it is time for him to arrive.

When I walk into the kitchen, where the guys are, I notice quickly that something is wrong. Both look mad and worried at the same time. Harsh breathing filters through the silence in the room. They are both staring at a bouquet of roses sitting in a clear vase on the table. Who are they for and who are they from?

"Whose flowers?" I ask, stepping closer to them.

Adam's hand shoots out to stop me. "Don't get any closer. They could be poisoned." *Poisoned?*

I eye him with a wary look. "You're scaring me, Adam. What's going on?"

He swallows hard, his gaze unwavering from the flowers. "These were left for you. They were sitting outside the door."

A shiver runs through me. "Who are they from?" Judging by Adam's tone of voice and the way he and Ethan continue to stare at the roses with mixed emotions gives me an idea.

"There is no card, but we have a pretty good idea." Adam backs away from the table, making his way to me. He pulls me against his chest, his hand creating soothing circles along my back.

"Why does he keep doing this?" I wonder aloud.

"I don't know, sweetheart. But it doesn't mean that our plans for today are ruined. Nothing is going to stop me from taking my girl out on a date." I have been looking forward to today ever since Adam mentioned that he was going to take me out. We haven't been out often because of past events and I feel bad about it.

"Are you sure it's okay?"

Adam reaches up and tucks a strand of hair behind my ear. "Trust me, where we are going, there will be lots of people and he wouldn't be stupid enough to do anything with that many people around." Adam seems so sure. I just hope he is right.

I put on a brave smile. "Well, I'm ready to go when you are."

He drops a kiss to my forehead, and then to my mouth. "Let's go have some fun, shall we?"

I walk over to Ethan, who meets me halfway, and hug him. I kiss his cheek before grabbing my phone, keys, and wallet off the coffee table. I link my arm through Adam's, ready to see what he has planned for the day.

The mall. Our first stop is the mall. I don't mind shopping, but when Adam or anyone else pays for my things, I don't like it.

"What are we doing here?"

"Shopping, what else do you do at a mall?"

I smack his arm playfully. "Crazy, you know what I mean."

"I'm taking you shopping for maternity clothes and then I am going to buy you some ice cream."

"Ice cream?" I ask in amazement. That sounds really good right now.

"Really? That's all you heard out of that?"

I smack him again. "Shut up, I'm pregnant. If you mention food, then that is all my brain registers."

Adam barks out a laugh and gets out of the truck.

"One outfit," I tell him as we are walking toward the entrance.

"Sure, sweetheart."

"I mean it, Adam. I don't like you buying my stuff. I'll have money soon so I can buy more then."

He pulls me to a stop and turns to face me. "We've been over this, Kaylee. I want to buy you things; you know this. One outfit is not going to be enough. All of your clothes are getting too small. Pretty soon, they won't fit at all."

"Thanks for reminding me," I grumble.

"I'll buy you all the ice cream you want if you let me get away with more than one outfit."

"That's not fair," I argue. I stare into his eyes and find that it is hard to tell him no. "Fine, but you can only get away with this one time."

He gives me a chaste kiss. "Thank you." He grabs my hand and pulls me along with him.

Two very long hours later, we are done and I finally get my ice cream. Adam ended up buying me four maternity shirts, two pairs a maternity pants— I drew the line at two—and a pair of leggings. I am not thrilled that he is spending so much money on me, but as long as he is happy, I'll deal with it.

"Where are we going next?"

"Are you up for bowling and mini golf?"

My face lights up with excitement. "Heck, yeah! I haven't been bowling or played mini golf in a long time."

We finish our ice cream and head to our next destination, Southern Lanes.

"I'm so going to kick your butt, babe," I taunt as Adam sets up the game.

"You want to wager that?"

"It depends on the wager."

"Whoever wins gets to pick where we go next."

Sounds simple. I hold out my hand to seal the deal. "You have a deal." He places his hand in mine and we shake on it.

Adam put me first so I pick up my little eight-pound ball and take my turn. The ball rolls down the lane knocking over six out of ten pins. I wait for the ball to return so I can go again. All of the remaining pins are close together so as long as I don't gutter it, I should get a spare. As I suspect, I knock all four pins down. I smile triumphantly at Adam and smack his butt when I walk by.

Adam laughs and grabs the ball he picked out. My smug grin fades when Adam's ball plows through all ten pins.

"What were you saying, sweetheart? Don't worry, I'll go easy on you," he says laughingly.

I narrow my eyes at him as I walk past him to take my turn. And I miss every stinking pin.

Adam and I continue the game, which turned into whoever concentrates the best wins since we were both trying to distract one another. Adam wins by twenty points, which explains why he is grinning smugly right now as we walk toward mini golf. "Are you ready to lose at this game, too?"

"We'll see. You sound so sure of yourself that you will win at this, too."

"I'm a pro at miniature golf, sweetheart. Watch and learn."

Halfway through the game, Adam is cursing under his breath for missing the shot for the third time on the tenth hole. "I thought I was supposed to be learning something?" I ask in a teasing tone.

"Shut up."

Night has fallen upon us by the time we leave mini golf. Obviously, I won. "Have you decided where we are going next?"

"Yep."

"You're not going to tell me, are you?"

He shakes his head. "Nope."

Adam drives a couple of miles down the road before pulling over and parking the truck near Fountain Square Park. It is always so beautiful this time of the year. I haven't actually been through it though. From what I have seen just passing by, it is breathtaking.

"Ready, sweetheart?"

"If we are going where I think we are going, then yes!" I clasp my hand with Adam's and almost squeal in delight when we head toward the entrance to the park.

"Oh Adam, it's so beautiful!" I can't help but be in awe of the scenery. Clear lights hang from every tree and every lamppost. Even the fountain is lit up tonight. Adam and I walk along the path toward the infamous fountain. He takes me by surprise, spinning me around, then tugging me toward him. He reaches into his pocket and pulls out his phone, snapping a picture of us.

Adam lets go of me and asks the lady next to us if she could take our picture. The lady smiles and takes his phone. Instead of just standing with my arms wrapped around him like I thought we were going to do, Adam surprises me, yet again, by dipping me and pressing his lips to mine. The moment ends all too soon and before I know it, we are standing upright again. Adam thanks her and pockets his phone.

I wrap my arms around his neck, lowering his head to mine. I'm dying to kiss him again. My fingers glide through his hair as he tugs on my lower lip with his teeth. "I love you so damn much, Kaylee Harper," Adam murmurs, his lips brushing mine.

"I love you more."

"Impossible."

# 10

*Adam*

*"For a while in the beginning, Riley made me believe he was different. Funny how someone's true colors show." –Kaylee*

Over the last week and a half, since Kaylee has been staying with her brother, I have been spending more time with Dad at the shop. I have missed our 'guy' time, and I know he has, too. Kaylee mentioned to me last night that Ethan is looking to move his car closer, and after talking with Dad, we are rearranging the shop so he can bring it in. He and Kaylee are on their way back to the car and should be here soon.

Christmas is in a few days and I have no earthly idea what to get her. Alexis says she's not hard to buy for, yet I can't think of a single thing. I did see this angel wing necklace a couple of days ago and I immediately thought of Kaylee. She mentioned a couple of months ago that for her eighteenth birthday she wanted to get a tattoo in memory of her father. She wanted angel wings around 'Daddy' on her right shoulder blade with the day he was born on the left wing and the day he passed away on the right wing. I debated whether or not to get the angel wing necklace, but now I think I'll go back and get it. I just hope it's still there. Now, I just need to think of another present.

Kaylee walks in the shop glowing, her smile so bright it's hard not to smile in return. She is wearing one the shirts I bought her when I took her shopping with a pair of sweatpants. You can definitely tell she is pregnant now. She is almost thirteen weeks and her belly has grown all of a sudden.

"Hey, sweetheart. I see you're feeling great today."
I pull her in for a long hug. I hope she moves back in with
me soon. I worry about her so much at night that I barely
sleep sometimes.

"I wasn't until about twenty minutes ago," she says,
and my mind starts wandering, coming up with scenarios
that could have happened. Is there another threat? Is she
having pains? Did they run into Riley or Elizabeth?

I usher her into Dad's office and make her sit down
in a chair. "Are you okay? What's wrong?"

She rolls her eyes like I'm being dramatic.
"Everything is fine, Adam. I have just been nauseated all
morning and nothing I do makes it go away."

Thank God, it was better than everything I was
coming up with. "Do you want to lay down?"

She shakes her head but stops suddenly, her hand
flying to her stomach. "Adam, they are kicking again!" She
hastily grabs my hands and places them on either side of
her belly.

Holy crap, that's amazing. "Wow," I whisper in
astonishment. "Dad! Come here!" He is going to want to
feel this.

The door to the shop swings open and Dad comes
barreling in. "What, son?"

"They're kicking, Dad." Dad smiles and I remove
one of my hands so he can feel.

Dad starts laughing. "You know, your mom is going
to be jealous that I got to be the first one to feel our
grandbabies kick."

I snort. "More like mad."

I hear Ethan hollering through the shop wondering
where everybody went. "In the office!" I yell so he can
hear.

Ethan walks in and stops. "They're already kicking
again, sis?"

I look up at Kaylee. "Again?"

"Yeah, I got to feel them almost twenty minutes ago," Ethan gloats. Well, dang, now I know how Mom is going to feel.

Dad stands and hugs Kaylee, thanking her.

When Dad lets go, I lean down and do the same, except I kiss her hard before letting go. "That was the most amazing thing, ever."

"Just wait until you get to see them, it's just as amazing."

Speaking of that. "When is your next appointment?"

Her face grows soft. "Sorry, I forgot to tell you. It's January 15th."

"When do we get to find out if they are boys or girls?" As long as they are healthy, I don't care what they are. Though, I have pictured having two little girls who look just like their momma.

"I don't think we will know until I'm eighteen weeks or so." Dang, that's still at least two months away. "Do you think maybe I can visit your mom later? I haven't seen her in what feels like weeks."

"Yeah, I'll take you to the house in a bit. Mom will be glad to see you." Mom keeps pestering me about having Kaylee visit. I keep telling her that I'll bring her by soon and I keep forgetting. No lie, Mom smacked me on the back of the head the last time I told her I forgot. I guess it worked because now I just made plans to bring Kaylee to the house. "I need to go back out there and help Dad, but if you need me all you have to do is yell and I'll come running, okay?" The sooner I get out there and help, the sooner I can go home and spend the evening with my girl.

She shoos me away. "Go, I'll be fine."

"Are you still feeling sick?"

"Not at the moment."

I let my lips fall to hers, the backs of my knuckles brushing her cheek. Every time I kiss her, I want more. Her lips are so soft and addictive; one taste is never enough.

"Adam! I need you out here, son!" Dad hollers from the shop.

I begrudgingly pull away and sigh. "I love you," I say as I kiss her one last time.

"Love you, too." That's all I need to get me through the day.

"Mom!" I holler when I enter the house.

"In the kitchen, sweetie!" I roll my eyes. I should have known that. She practically stays in there.

I bring Kaylee's hand up to my mouth and kiss the back of it as we make our way to the kitchen or Mom's sanctuary. However you want to put it.

Mom is at the stove, her back to us, stirring what smells like chili. "Dinner's almost ready. Is your father here, yet?" Mom finally turns around and gasps when she sees Kaylee next to me. "Oh my, it's so good to see you!" Mom exclaims as she walks over to us, pulling Kaylee in for a long hug. "I've been telling Adam that he needs to bring you by to see me."

"I've missed you, Anna. I asked him earlier if he could bring me by and well, here I am."

"How is everything going? Still have morning sickness?" Mom asks Kaylee, and they talk for the next twenty minutes about pregnancy. "Oh dear, I almost forgot. This letter came for you, sweetie." Mom pulls an envelope out of her purse and hands it to her. Kaylee studies the envelope with curiosity. I watch as she opens it and reads the letter.

I am trying not to be nosy because I know if she wants me to know, she'll tell me, but when her expression falls, I can't resist asking. "What does it say, sweetheart?"

"The trial…it's been pushed back," she says with so much sadness.

Anger pulses through my veins. "What do you mean it's been pushed back?" I look at Mom and ask, "Can they do that?"

"I'm afraid so, Adam. Kaylee, does it say why?"

Kaylee looks up from the parchment. "It says that Riley was granted permission to postpone the trial because of lawyer issues."

"How long did they postpone it?"

"Until the January 26th." Two weeks. They pushed the trial back two weeks so now she's going to have to endure seeing him at school longer. I hate this for her. I wrap my arms around her and she lays her head on my chest, my chin resting on top of her head.

"I think I'm going to go lie down for a bit," she whispers in my shirt.

"Are you not hungry, sweetheart?"

"No."

I exhale, my hands running up and down her back. "Kaylee, you need to eat."

"I'm not hungry."

I kiss her hair. "Okay, want me to go with you?"

"No, I just want to be alone for a bit."

"I love you," I tell her 'cause I think she needs to hear it.

She gives me a weak smile. "Love you, too." I watch her walk to my room and close the door behind her before pulling out a chair and plopping in it. I bury my head in my hands and breathe in deeply. It seems we can never catch a break where Riley is concerned.

A hand touches my back. "I'm sorry, sweetie. Just give her some time to process this. She's strong, remember that."

I turn and stare at my bedroom door. I want to go in there and hold her, comfort her, because I bet my life she's crying, but I also want to give her the space she asks for. I hate knowing that she is upset and I can't do anything about it.

My phone vibrates in my pocket so I pull it out and check my messages.

**Kaylee:** *I need you*

That one text, those three words, is all I need to hear. I jump up from my seat and walk briskly to my room.

I close the door quietly behind me and take off my shoes before climbing into bed with her. She turns over so she's facing me. Her eyes are red, tear-filled. She immediately snuggles closer to me, her hands fisting my shirt. I whisper soothing thoughts to her and rub her back, trying to keep her calm.

"Can I stay with you tonight?" My heart soars at her question. On the inside, I'm smiling so big at the thought of her being in my arms all night.

"Sweetheart, you never have to ask."

It isn't long before her breathing evens out and she's fast asleep. Her hands have loosened their grip on my shirt some, her head in the crook of my neck. I tighten my arms around her, needing her closer.

Tonight, I get to hold my girl all night long. Nothing can top that.

## Kaylee

*"I am trying to do everything I can to break free from the devil's clutches, but they are always one step ahead."-Riley*

I snuggle against the warmth that envelops me. Feather-like kisses rain over my forehead, my cheek, my nose, and finally, my mouth. I smile against Adam's lips and kiss him deeply.

"Hmm…I've missed this, sweetheart," Adam croons softly.

I have missed this, too. Staying at Ethan's is helping me learn to stand on my own two feet, though. I was relying too much on Adam to take away the pain and the terrors when, in reality, all I was doing was stalling. I wasn't healing at the rate I thought I was. But now I feel like I'm almost where I want to be. I plan to stay with Ethan, with the exception of tonight, for the duration of Christmas break. I enjoy our time together and I have missed not getting to see or talk to my brother for four long years. Even when I thought he blamed me for what happened to Dad, I still wanted to call him so I could hear his voice. But I was afraid of what he might say at the time so I would chicken out. I wish I'd had the guts to call him so we could have reconciled sooner. What's done is done and I can't change the past; all I can do is move forward.

"Just think, soon I will be here every night for you to hold." I was surprised that Adam took it as well as he did when I told him my decision. He's so understanding; that's another reason why I love him.

He groans. "You're killing me, sweetheart."

I was going to reply, but my stomach decided to growl, ruining our moment. I face plant into his chest and giggle. I feel his body vibrate from laughter, which only made me laugh harder.

"I guess that means I need to feed you," he jokes. He pulls away and kisses my forehead before climbing out of the bed. "Chili okay?"

"Yeah, sounds good." He walks out of his room and I start searching for my phone. I need to text Ethan and let him know I'm staying with Adam tonight. I find it sitting on the nightstand. Adam must've moved it while I was asleep.

I tap my messages icon and select Ethan's thread.

**Me: Hey bro, I'm going to stay with Adam tonight.**

He replies almost instantly.

**Ethan: Okay what time should I come pick you up tomorrow?**

Well, that was easy. I'm surprised he didn't ask why.

**Me: I'm not sure. I'll text you when I know.**
**Ethan: K**

Adam returns with my chili and some tea. Adam picks a movie for us to watch and pops it in. He slides back under the covers with me and we sit with our backs resting against the headboard, his arm around my shoulders, while I eat my chili.

I sigh blissfully and lean my head against Adam's shoulder, feeling happier than ever before.

## Alexis

I'm currently parked outside Ethan's apartment complex, fixing to surprise Kaylee with a girls' night. I grab my bag from the seat beside me and step out into the bitter cold. I can't wait for spring to get here. Cold weather and I do not get along. A chill runs up my spine, causing me to hug my arms. None of the guys know I came alone. I seriously think they are overreacting to the threat, but you can't tell them that or they go all crazy on you. I like that they care enough about me to want to protect me, but I'm beginning to suffocate.

I knock on the door and wait...and wait. I am about to knock again when the door cracks open. When Ethan sees it's me, he opens it a little wider. I gulp at the sight of him. He's shirtless, displaying his perfectly sculpted abs. His shorts hang loose on his hips. My mouth suddenly feels dry. Perspiration mattes his face and drips from his hair, looking as if he just stepped out of the shower.

"What are you doing here, Lex, especially alone?" he growls.

I purse my lips. "I came to surprise Kaylee with a girls' night."

He curses and drags me inside his apartment, shutting the door behind us. "First of all, Kaylee is staying with Adam tonight. Secondly, you know you're not supposed to going anywhere alone."

"Screw the rules, Ethan. I don't think they apply to me." I turn to walk out the door, but Ethan's arm shoots out, stopping me.

"I'm taking you home and there will be no ifs, ands, or butts about it. Does Brad know that you're alone?"

"No, he thinks you and Kaylee picked me up."

His eyes shut briefly, as he blows out a breath. "Don't go nowhere. Let me get my keys and I will run you home." He lets go of my arm and walks to his room. The door shuts quietly behind him and I'm left standing, wondering what he is doing.

I freeze when I hear the same whiny voice from the other night. My stomach churns at the thought of them together. Suddenly, I need air. I walk outside into the frigid air and breathe. My heart shouldn't be breaking in two right now, but it is and it sure as hell is painful. Why, I'm not sure because I tell myself he's not worth it, that he is not the one for me. Why won't my heart listen?

I force my legs to take me to my car. I am halfway down the stairs when Ethan comes barreling out of his apartment. "What do you think you're doing?"

Against my better judgment, I stop and turn. I shouldn't look at him, knowing I'm on the verge tears. I'm pissed at myself for getting upset over something stupid. "I'm going home."

He's standing on the step above me, towering over me. "I thought we discussed that I am taking you home?"

I reach up and jab his chest with my index finger. "No, you made that decision! I'm perfectly capable of driving home alone so if you don't mind I'd like to leave. I'm sure your conquest for the night is waiting for you." I don't wait for him to respond. Spinning on my heels, I continue down the stairs and make a beeline for my car.

I let out a squeal when my feet leave the pavement. "Put me down, Ethan, right now or so help me I will stab you!" I bang my fists against his back though it doesn't seem to faze him.

He drops me in the passenger seat of his truck and I let out a huff, crossing my arms. Pissed does not even begin to describe how I feel right now. Livid is more like it.

"Do you need me to buckle you or can you manage?"

I narrow my eyes at him and jerk the seat belt from his hands. He is so infuriating. "I've got it," I ground out.

Ethan holds his hands up in surrender as he backs away and walks around to the driver's side and climbs in.

Not a word is said as Ethan turns onto the highway. I'm coming up with different ways to kill him in my mind. How dare he go all caveman and force me into his truck?!

"What about my car?"

"Don't worry about it. I will get it to you tomorrow." I can tell by his tone that I should leave it at that.

I open an app on my phone and start playing the newest game I'm addicted to, Trivia Crack. "Crap, I knew that," I mutter under my breath when I pick the wrong answer.

"I could've told you the answer was California," Ethan says laughingly.

I glare at him. "You're supposed to be driving, not paying attention to what I'm doing." I shrink closer to the door and open my Facebook app. I'm scrolling through my newsfeed and stop briefly when I see a friend of mine posted a picture of a shirtless guy. He is gorgeous, but not as good looking as the guy who is driving me home. *I need to quit thinking of Ethan and his good looks,* I scold myself inwardly.

A low growl rumbles from the driver's seat. "Are you okay?" I ask bitterly.

"Does Brad know you look at half naked guys?"

Okay, I've had it with him. "Number one, I don't need to explain anything to you. Number two, you should not be paying attention to what I'm doing. I want to make it home in one piece! How do you know what I'm looking at anyway? You can't even see my screen!"

"The glare from your phone is reflecting in the window," he simply states.

I huff and lock my screen, setting it on my lap. Crossing my arms, I lay my head against the window. I wish he wasn't so infuriating then I might even like him. Who am I kidding, I do like him, and that's the problem. I probably even like him too much.

The fact that my plans fell through for the night has me bummed. I was looking forward to spending time with Kaylee, but I know she needs her time with Adam. She deserves to be happy and I'm proud of how far she has come. When I met her, I didn't expect us to become friends. She wasn't the type of person I usually hung around with. I smile to myself as I think back to the day the teacher assigned us to work on the same project. I wasn't happy about her being my partner, but in the end, I wouldn't change a moment of our friendship.

I pick up my phone and tap the messages icon. I text Brad, hoping he doesn't have plans for tonight. I don't want to sit home and be bored. Plus, if I want to try and have a relationship with him, then this will be a good night to start.

**Me: Hey, I'm on my way home, Kaylee is going to Adam's. Wanna do something?**

Surprisingly, he replies right away.

**Brad: Yeah, be there in a few. What do you have in mind?**

I take a moment to think of something.

**Me: Are you hungry? We can do Chinese takeout and a movie.**

**Brad: Sounds like a plan. See you soon, babe.**

Brad is everything a girl could ask for. He's romantic, he's a sweetheart, and he is really outgoing. I really wish I felt more for him. He is so sweet to me, and I know he deserves better than a girl who is pining over another guy.

Ethan pulls into my driveway and I cross my fingers, hoping Brad hasn't arrived yet. He knows Kaylee is with Adam, but he won't like seeing me with Ethan, alone. Ethan could also rat me out to Brad. I don't think he will, though I don't want a chance for that to happen.

I sigh in relief when I don't see Brad's truck.

The moment that Ethan puts the truck in park, I open my door and jump out without so much as a good-bye. I wasn't about to thank him for the ride I never asked for. If Brad asks where my car is, I won't know what to tell him. I've already lied once to him and that shouldn't have happened. If he asks, then I guess I will put on my big girl panties and deal with it.

"Lex, wait," Ethan hollers as he steps out of his truck. I slow to a stop and spin around slowly. I love and hate that he calls me Lex. I don't open my mouth to say anything. I just wait for him to say what he wants. His large hand runs over his head in agitation. "I…have a good night." I stand there, frozen in place. That's it?

Ethan abruptly turns and gets back in his truck. I spin on my heels and march the rest of the way to my front door, damning Ethan Harper and his ability to play with my emotions the whole way. I head straight for the bathroom to try to cover up the evidence before Brad arrives. I touch up my make-up and throw my hair up in a ponytail. I change out my jeans and sweater for a silky pajama set.

The doorbell chimes so I rush to answer the door. Brad's smiling face and a bouquet of roses greet me from the other side.

"Aww…Brad, these are beautiful! You didn't have to get me these!" I throw my arms around his neck, hugging him hard. When I release him, his lips find mine for the sweetest kiss. I let out a giggle when he dips me, kissing me harder.

We straighten and I pull away from him to go arrange the roses in a vase.

Brad comes up behind me, placing his hands on my hips. "What do you want to eat and I'll order it." My hearts speeds up a little from his touch. See, I'm not totally immune to the romantic that is Brad Massey.

I give him my order and wait as he calls and places the order for our food. We pick out a movie and settle on my bed, cuddling with each other as the previews start.

Brad goes and gets the food when it arrives, and we sit on my bed and eat. The movie is suddenly forgotten when Brad tries to feed me some of his chicken. We laugh when it slips through his chopsticks and lands on my lap.

We cut up and laugh about the craziest things the rest of the evening. Brad may not make my heart race as fast as Ethan can, but he can still put butterflies in my stomach and a smile on my face.

*Kaylee*

*"It hurts when I'm continuously reminded of all the things my father will miss out on in my life."–Kaylee*

Normally, I don't celebrate Christmas since I hadn't had a reason to, but this year I am eager to spend it with Adam and his parents, my best friend, who is practically my sister, and my brother. Next year, I will have two new reasons to celebrate. I can't help but smile just thinking about it. Honestly, I didn't presume I'd be this excited about being a mother so soon. With Adam not hesitating to take on the fatherly role and with the support I have from his parents, Ethan and, of course, my best friend, why shouldn't I be excited. Anna and Jack are already calling them their grandkids. I'm still hung up on the fact that I'm having twins. You know what they say, two is better than one.

I wasn't expecting any presents, but Anna and Jack bought me the pregnancy bible, *What to Expect When You're Expecting,* and two gender-neutral baby books. Adam bought me a Pandora bracelet with a charm that says 'mommy' and another one in a shape of a heart with our birthstones in it. He also bought me a breathtaking necklace. It is a gold angel wing necklace. I almost cried when I opened the velvet box that it was in.

Alexis bought me a couple of maternity shirts. The first one is white and in black writing it says, "I'm having twins. What's your excuse?" The other shirt is black with two white conversation bubbles. The first bubble says, "Ha-ha, I just kicked her ribs." The second bubble says,

"Cool…my turn!" We all cracked up at that one. Finally, Ethan bought me two silver eight-by-ten picture frames that have thirteen small circles so I can add a picture every month to see how much they change as they grow.

All in all, it was the best Christmas I'd had in years.

Ethan and I walk along the familiar trail through the cemetery to see Dad while the crisp winter air hits my face. This is the first time we have been together to see Dad. I'm sure he is grinning ear to ear right now, watching us.

"I remember the last time you were here. I stood back watching while you visited Dad, you know to give you some space, and I remember wanting to walk up and talk to you. I decided not to because I didn't think it was the right time to do it." He laughs softly before continuing. "Plus, Alexis and Adam were shooting daggers through me already so it would have caused an even bigger scene. I'm glad they're protective of you, though." I wrack my brain trying to remember if they had mentioned it to me, but I come up with nothing.

"They didn't say a word to me about you being there." Why did they keep that from me?

"Probably because I looked like a creeper and they didn't want to worry you." I giggle as I imagine the looks on their faces.

"Honestly, I probably looked like a stalker because I guess you were in the hospital at the time when I showed up at your house wanting to talk to you. Alexis opened the door and threatened to call the cops on me. Then, of course, one month later, I was on my way to see if you were home and I spotted you at Mancino's."

"You and your stalker-like ways," I tease.

We stay and talk to Dad for a while, sharing stories. Ethan mainly tells stories of us that he remembers, and others of him and Dad. Mine are all of Dad and me; I only told a couple of Ethan and me, since he already told all the good ones.

The sun is setting when we tell Dad that we'll visit him again soon. I hate saying good-bye. Saying good-bye means that I'm not coming back. I don't want our time together to end yet, but I am freezing and the last thing I need is to be sick. I hope we can do this again soon, though.

"Can I ask you something?" Ethan asks curiously, as he helps me to the car. I swear, what is it with people thinking that I'm fragile?

"Sure. What's on your mind?"

"How in the hell did you and Alexis meet because you two are total opposites, just saying."

I burst out laughing at his admission.

I wait for him to climb in the car so I can answer him. "Well, we met freshman year. Our teacher made us partners for a project she assigned. At first, we didn't like each other. I mean, she was the outgoing, stuck-up type, and I was the shy, quiet type. I just felt comfortable around her and the more we talked, the more we became friends. I realized she wasn't who I thought she was." He doesn't answer; he just simply nods. "Why do you ask?" Again, he doesn't answer; he just shrugs his shoulders, though he does have sort of a smile on his face. "If you like her, just ask her out."

He gives me the how-do-you-know look before saying, "I can't." My brow furrows waiting for him to elaborate. He finally sighs, noticing that I'm not giving up. "I'm probably going to get shipped out in a year, and I don't want a relationship with her because I don't want to promise her things when I may not be able to fulfill them. Besides, I'm too old for her anyway." Excuses, excuses. At least the being too old for her line is. It's not like he is ten years her senior. I sort of understand the rest, but love doesn't wait forever. The thought of Ethan shipping out in a year saddens me, but it is his job.

"Ethan, I'm going to be honest with you. First of all, you are not too old for her. I mean, she is about to turn eighteen soon. Secondly, I understand where you're coming from, but what happens when you come back and she's with someone else? I mean other than Brad because, let's face it, I seriously doubt those two will last much longer. But don't tell her I said that. Would you be able to handle seeing her with someone else? You will regret it for the rest of your life because you did nothing. Surely, you want to have someone to come home to?" Brad is an awesome guy and a wonderful friend, but I just can't see him and Alexis together. I don't think she is into him as much as he thinks.

"I'll have you and the babies to welcome me home." He puts the truck in park and cuts the engine.

"That's not what I mean and you know it." Instead of answering, he just gets out and opens the door for me. "So you're not going to answer me now because I'm right?"

He stops walking and gazes at me for a second. "I don't want to be responsible for breaking her heart if something happens."

I pull him into a hug. I can't believe we are talking about this. "If it were me, I'd be thankful for the times we had. Sure, I'd be heartbroken, but I would do it all over again even though I'd know the outcome. Why are we even discussing this anyway? You are going to come home." I look up at him and immediately wished I hadn't because I can see the fear in his eyes.

"Everything okay?" I turn in the direction of Alexis's voice. I drop my arms and give him a look. The look that says 'just think about it.'

"Yeah, we were just talking," I answer her. I hope she doesn't do her usual 'ask until we finally spill' inquisition. I know she can tell something is up, but it's not my place to tell her. If he wants her, then he is going to have to grow a pair and ask her out himself.

An uncomfortable silence forms as we walk inside. I wish they would just figure out what they want and go for it. I know from experience that you shouldn't ignore your feelings. If Brad is who she wants, then she needs to focus on him. If it's Ethan, then she needs to let Brad go and she and Ethan should quit doing whatever they are doing. Maybe later I can pull her aside and see if she wants to talk.

I kept pushing Adam away when I should have been running to him. Maybe he could have saved me from being at Riley's mercy. I shake my head, not wanting to go there. I need to quit thinking about the past and focus on my future. Staying in the past is what is keeping me from healing. Adam and the twins are my future.

As if he knows I'm thinking about him, he turns and smiles warmly at me. I walk over to him and wrap my arms around his waist, wanting the feel his love around me. I sigh, feeling content when his arms embrace me.

"Did you have a good visit?" he asks in my hair. I smile and nod against his chest.

Right here, right now, at this moment, only makes me love him more, if that's even possible. Tears prick my eyes and I want to laugh.

Darn hormones.

A few days later, I pack up my belongings from Ethan's apartment. Tomorrow, school resumes and I will be back with Adam and his parents until graduation. I'm not looking forward to tomorrow, although I am looking forward to sharing a bed with Adam again. I will miss getting to see my brother on a daily basis, but I'm ready to cuddle with Adam. Basketball resumes for him and I'm happy that I will get to see him play the game we love. He mentioned a few days ago that he wanted to quit again. I told him that I wanted him to finish out his senior season and that he shouldn't quit what he loves just for me. He is worried about me and I love that he is, but he only has like three weeks left in the season so he might as well finish it out.

Ｗe have another session with Dr. Lawson tonight that I'm also nervous about. I hope this session goes better than the last.

Adam picks me up from Ethan's early enough so we have time to run through the drive thru somewhere and pick up some food before we head to our appointment.

I know that we are more than likely going to pick up where we left off from our last visit so I am slightly better prepared to answer. Right now, I feel pretty confident that I can talk about Riley and what he did to me, but it may change when the time comes. I feel like I need to get it off my chest tonight; like it's the only thing left holding me back.

Tonight, I will finally break free of Riley's hold.

Tonight will be the night I freely talk about my rape and assault.

## Kaylee

*"Who knew my heart could hold so much indecision?"- Alexis*

"Adam, Kaylee. It's nice to see you two back," Dr. Lawson greets us when we walk in her office. She stands and shakes our hands before motioning us to sit. "I hope you have had a good week so far. Tell me, what has happened over the last two weeks? Anything new you want to share?"

My eyes drop to the floor and my fingers knot in my lap. I can feel her gaze on me. Maybe I should just go ahead and get it over with? If I do that, I don't want to spend the whole hour discussing it. Then again, if I wait, I may chicken out.

"Kaylee, anything you want to share?" I look up and meet her eyes. She knows there is something to share; I can tell by the way that she is assessing me.

"Um, yes, actually." My pulse picks up its pace as the nervousness of what I am about to do takes over. I look nervously at Adam. Do I really want him to hear this again? I know he is here for me, yet I know talking about it has to bother him.

As if she can read my mind, Dr. Lawson asks, "Would you like for Adam to wait outside?"

Surprise registers on his face when I nod.

"I'll just be right outside if you need me," he murmurs and kisses my cheek.

When Adam closes the door behind him, I suddenly start to wonder why I wanted him to wait outside. No, I need to do this on my own. I've battled my nightmares so I can do this.

"You can start whenever you're ready, Kaylee. Just take your time," she coaches.

I take a couple of slow, deep breaths, trying to keep myself from freaking out. *I can do this*, I tell myself a few times.

I swallow hard and begin my story. "Um, back in May, I started dating this guy named Riley. He had been asking me out all school year and I kept turning him down. I could tell he wasn't going to give up so I said yes to one date. One date turned into two, and after that, he asked me to be his girlfriend and I said yes. Over the summer, things were amazing, but he started to change toward the end when school was fixing to start up again. I brushed it off and went on, thinking he was just upset about something.

"The first time he hit me, I was waiting for him to come to my house after practice. He came bursting through the door and automatically punched me. He stomped on my leg and threatened to end my senior season of basketball if I went out with Adam behind his back again."

I continue with my story, talking about him knocking me down the stairs and the wreck that followed. I tell her about how he claimed I couldn't hang out with my best friend because she was a "bad influence," yet when I was around her, he would never do anything about it. I tell Dr. Lawson everything I let happen.

I pause when I reach the part that has scarred me the most. The lump in my throat grows and my hands start to shake. I breathe in and exhale slowly a couple of times, trying to find the courage to continue. I've come this far, so I believe I can push through and get it all out.

I start off strong, and I slow when I get closer to the worst part of it all. I push myself to get through the part where he took my innocence. It hurts knowing that someone takes a part of you, a part you can never get back, just because they think it's a thrill. Riley knew I was clinging to it with all my might. He tried hard on occasions, begged me at times, to let him take me. He promised he would be slow and gentle, that he would take care of me. Nothing about that night was gentle. I'm happy I didn't freely give in to him because it wouldn't have meant jack to him.

A tear, one lone tear, slips down my cheek. That is all I shed for what he's done to me now. It feels amazing to care less about the traumatic situations you went through. It will always be a part of me, and I know there will be times when I reflect on the past, but I will no longer feel like someone is taking a knife to my soul.

I am so close to being the carefree person I want to be. My father's murder is behind me; now all I need to do is finish pushing Riley behind me.

Dr. Lawson is smiling at me by the time I'm done. "I'm very proud of you, Kaylee. How do you feel now? Better?"

"Surprisingly," I admit. "Can Adam come back in now?"

"If you want him to." She stands and goes to let Adam know that he can come back in.

He sits next me and drapes his arm around my shoulders.

"Thank you for joining us, Adam. I was just telling Kaylee here how proud of her I am. I do have one question though, Kaylee, if you don't mind. Why did you want Adam to sit outside?"

I reach over and place my hand on Adam's leg. "I felt like it was something I needed to do alone. Over the last two weeks, I have been staying with my brother and have been trying to deal with the nightmares I have. I realized one day that I relied on Adam to help me get through, and while he helped me at the time, I never felt it was a step closer to where I wanted to be. If I wanted to get to where I wanted to be, then I would have to do it on my own. That was why I had Adam step outside. I felt I needed to face my past on my own. Plus, I know it has to bother him to hear it."

"Right you are, Kaylee. When we rely on others, we never learn to stand on our own two feet. Adam, does it bother you to hear Kaylee or someone else talk about it?"

"In a way, yes, because all you see are these images of what she's saying and it hurts to know that I dropped her off and left her there. I think of all the 'what ifs,' all the scenarios that could have happened, and wonder why I didn't do something different. I just feel like I should have picked up on the signs and stopped it, you know?" My heart hurts to hear him say that, in a roundabout way, he feels he is to blame.

"That is quite an assumption, Adam. Oftentimes we like to think if we could have done things differently that the outcome of the situation would be better. In reality, most of the time, it may not. You wouldn't know if Riley would have accomplished what he did if you, let's say, picked up on what was happening and tried to stop it. The outcome could have been either he would have gotten to her sooner and hurt her worse or he would have chickened out and left her alone. You don't want to be stuck in the past with all of the 'what ifs' in life because you will be there for the rest of your life wondering. The past is not a good place to be."

No, it isn't. I've only recently begun to learn that.

"I want the two of you to try something over the next couple of weeks. I want you both to focus only on the days ahead of you instead of the days behind you. Can you do that for me?"

Adam and I nod in agreement. "When I see you in two weeks, I want you to tell me how different you feel. All right? Wonderful session today, Kaylee. I'll see you two in two weeks."

We say our good-byes and leave her office. The drive to the house is short, which is unfortunate for me since I want this night to drag on. The longer I have to put off going to school tomorrow, the better. I don't know if Riley will show up tomorrow or not, but let's hope not.

I change out of my sweats, slipping into my pajamas before crawling into bed. Adam is right behind me, curling his arm around me and scooting me back so his chest is pressing against my back.

"Sleep tight, sweetheart." His lips find my neck, placing an open mouth kiss against my sensitive skin. I snuggle closer to him, relishing the feel of his warm body against mine. "Kaylee…" he warns in a tight voice. I freeze, aware of the problem I am creating for him.

"Sorry," I reply, trying not to laugh.

"Uh-huh, sure you are. I think you know exactly what you're doing." He kisses the sweet spot behind my ear, heating up my body. It's been a while since Adam's made love to me. It's not that we haven't wanted to; we just haven't had the chance. I want to rectify the situation right now.

I roll over so I am facing him. My chest is pressing against his, our legs tangle together, and our mouths an inch from one another. I slip my hand under his shirt, wanting to feel his skin beneath my fingertips. A small groan releases from his throat as he attacks my mouth. I let my fingers continue to graze his tan skin, trailing my fingers up and then back down again.

"You're killing me, sweetheart," he says in a hoarse voice.

I gaze longingly at him, memorizing the loving look in his face. There is so much attraction and desire in his eyes when he looks at me. At times when he prolongs his gaze, I want to hide my face from his scrutiny.

Adam leans forward, breaking eye contact, to kiss the hollow of my throat. I tilt my head back, giving him more access. My hands find his hair, tugging it gently.

As the night goes on, he kisses, touches, and rocks me into oblivion more than once. I curl into him, wearing only his shirt and my underwear, with a smile plastered on my sweaty face, feeling sated.

"It always gets better with you, Kaylee. Sweet dreams, sweetheart," he croons softly.

My hand cups the back of his neck, bringing his face down to mine for one last long, slow kiss. "Thank you for loving me and for being here with me."

"As I've told you before, I wouldn't want to be anywhere else. You are my world, Kaylee Harper. I'm never going to let you go." His arms enclose around me, holding me to him.

I sigh happily. "Good, 'cause without you, I'd be lost in this horrible world." Lost is putting it mildly. I'd be floating in a sea of darkness, struggling to keep my head above the surface if it wasn't for Adam.

Adam shakes his head in disbelief. "I don't believe that, sweetheart. It may take you a while, but eventually, you would have found your way. You have so much strength and determination packed into this beautiful body of yours. But we will never know for sure because I'll always be by your side, holding your hand. You'll never be alone again."

"You have too much faith in me."

"Nonsense, Kaylee. Believe it."

"Okay, Adam," I say just to agree.

"One day, Kaylee, I'll get you to see your worth."

"If you say so."

## Kaylee

*"I just want to run to her and confess it all and beg until she forgives me. Both parts of that statement will never happen though because I can't confess to her just yet. No amount of begging will make her forgive me, and I don't blame her."- Riley*

I stare openly at the clock on the nightstand in front of me. Seconds, minutes tick by, inching closer to when I have to crawl out of bed and go to school. Today is our first day back from Christmas break, and I'm so not looking forward to walking those shady halls again. Graduation is just a few, seemingly long, months away and it seems to be taking its precious time. I'm like a snail trying to reach its destination. I have been tossing and turning all night, dreading the morning when I will have to crawl out of bed to get ready for the hell that I know will be waiting for me.

The alarm sounds and I jump at the shrill sound. I knew it was coming, yet I still flinched. I stretch my arm out and hit the snooze button. Adam stirs behind me, rolling over to wrap his arm my mid-section.

"Morning, sweetheart," he rasps in my ear.

"Morning," I say quietly, unable to hide the disdain in my voice.

He nudges me back so I turn to face him. "Someone will always be with you, Kaylee. He won't touch you; I won't let him get that close."

"It's not just him who I'm worried about," I murmur honestly. I'm not naive to think that my classmates will be nice to me just because I'm pregnant. That only exists in a perfect world. If only there was such a thing.

"Screw them, Kaylee. They are jealous because you are breathtaking and happy. Don't let them steal what you have been searching for. You deserve it, not them."

"How do you always know just what to say to make me feel better?"

"It's a gift," he says jokingly, and we both laugh. "How about it, sweetheart? You ready to show everyone how little you care about what they think?"

"Let's do this," I say with a sudden burst of confidence.

"That's my girl."

I take my time getting ready, not caring if we are late. I settle for a pair of blue jeans, a t-shirt, and my basketball hoodie. I tie the laces on my tennis shoes and pull my hair back in a loose ponytail. After one last look in the mirror, I head downstairs to eat my breakfast. I hope Adam warned Anna not to cook any eggs. I'd rather not start my morning off with my head in the toilet. Thankfully, when I round the corner, the sweet smell of pancakes hit me. My stomach growls in approval.

"Here she is," Anna beams like they have been waiting a while for me.

"It's about time; I was fixing to send out a search party," Adam jokes.

"Sorry, I was just taking my time this morning."

"No problem, sweetie. Now eat up, and if you want more, don't hesitate to ask." She winks at me as she places three round, mouthwatering pancakes on my plate.

At precisely seven-thirty, Adam and I are on our way to hell, aka, school. Adam continues to reassure me that it will be okay. He has more faith in humanity than I do. I don't foresee today or any day at school going well. Kids are cruel, there's no doubt about it. The girls like to stick you with their claws and rip your confidence to shreds. The guys just like to taunt and make sick jokes to make you feel like you're nothing. If the judge hadn't ordered me to stay in school, I would have dropped out already. I would just get my GED and be done with it. Simple, right? I wish, but the only reason the judge granted me the emancipation from my mother is because I promised her that I would stay in school. When I weigh my options, the emancipation from my mother outweighs dropping out of school, so I guess I will have to suck it up and deal with it.

When I step out of Adam's truck, I immediately grab his hand. "Relax, Kaylee. Everything will be okay, sweetheart." He removes his hand from mine, letting his arm circle my waist. His lips brush my temple and I lean into him.

He keeps his arm locked around my waist as we walk into school. I try to focus on Adam's hand on my hip instead of the looks I'm getting. Why can't they leave me alone? I don't understand why people want to bully others. What is the point of it?

I make Adam open my locker door since I'm afraid to. My last first day back, Riley left me a 'welcoming' note. I turn and rest my forehead against his chest as he opens my locker door.

My body locks up when I hear Adam curse under his breath. What did Riley do now?

"Kaylee, I hate to say this, but he is on his way over here. Just ignore whatever he says. He won't get close enough to touch you, I won't let him."

I squeeze my eyes shut, hoping to block out Riley and his mocking voice. It's a long shot, I know, but I know I can't see his face without remembering the night he stole my innocence.

"Don't worry, babe, I didn't leave a note this time if that's what you're thinking. I thought I might welcome you in person this time."

I clench Adam's shirt in my hands and grit my teeth. Why can't he just walk away?

"Just walk away, Thompson. I don't have a problem knocking your teeth in," Adam threatens.

"What? I'm just being a nice classmate by welcoming my fellow classmates back. No harm in that, right?"

Suddenly, all the pent-up stress, worry, and frustration bubbles over. I spin around, surprising Adam and myself by taking a couple of steps forward toward the one person who destroyed my happiness. "You, aren't worth the shit on someone's shoe, Riley. I don't care how rich your family is, I don't care what tricks you have up your sleeve, and I don't care how many people you have behind you kissing your ass, you will pay for what you did to me!" My chest heaves, drawing in a much-needed breath. Man, it felt good to get that off my chest. All around us, people gasp.

Adam grabs my arm and tugs me back so his chest is against my back.

Shock registers on Riley's face for a brief second but fades instantly back to his malicious smirk. I try to keep my cool and remain confident. I don't want him to think if he just looks at me that I will crumple.

"You see, that's where you are wrong, *sweetheart*," he says mocking Adam's endearment for me. "It's all about who you have in your pocket and I have the judge and the jury right here." He pats his pocket with a smug grin.

"Bring it, asshole, 'cause I'm not afraid of you anymore."

He throws his head back and laughs and the people around us do the same. He leans forward and I fight the urge to flinch back. "I'd be very afraid if I were you. You haven't seen all I'm capable of."

Adam steps around me, putting himself between Riley and me. "And I suggest you walk away before I follow through with my previous threat."

"Fine, I will walk away, for now at least. But, know this, I am far from finished."

I duck behind Adam, digging my nails into his biceps when Riley's cold, dead eyes stare directly at me. He marches away down the hall, his posse on his heels.

Adam spins around and hugs me tight. "I'm not going to lie, sweetheart, seeing you stand up to him is such a turn on."

I laugh at his audacity. "Good to know."

"Kaylee!" Alexis yells, fighting through the crowded hallway, dragging Brad along behind her. "Did I seriously miss it?!"

"It wasn't much of a show."

"Baby girl, you standing up to someone as disgusting as him is the show!"

I wave her off and grab my books from my locker.

Today has already started off horribly. I hope that the rest of the day gets better.

The first four classes pass smoothly without any more hiccups, unless you count the sneers and the death glares constantly thrown my way. I'm sitting in my last class of the day, trying not to puke. I don't know if it's nerves from Riley sitting a few down from me or if it is the morning sickness kicking in. I don't understand why they call it 'morning sickness' when it lasts all day sometimes.

Thankfully, my teachers and I have an understanding; if I feel at any time I need to run to the bathroom, I can go, no questions asked. Which explains why I am running out of the room right now with my hand over my mouth to the nearest bathroom. I've gone all day without feeling sick and now, all of a sudden, during the last ten minutes of school, I throw up.

I am washing my hands when the bell rings so I quickly dry my hands off and head out in the hallway. Maybe Brad thought to grab my stuff when he left class. The traffic in the hallway is brutal, as usual. I pretty much have to fight my way through. Suddenly, someone pushes me from behind into the person in front of me. I start to apologize to the person I ran into, but they push me right back.

"Whore!" a girl shouts.

"Slut!" a guy yells as I'm lurched forward again.

I try to regain my footing, except I'm not fast enough and I find myself shoved in the opposite direction. I try to block out their cruel words, but they break through regardless, taunting me.

Familiar arms fly around me from behind, stopping my descent to whichever direction I am headed. "I got you," Adam murmurs in my ear. I turn in his hold, laying my head on his chest.

Alexis steps in my line of vision, looking furious. "What is wrong with all of you?! She is pregnant, for goodness' sakes! If you want to beat up somebody, why don't you beat the hell out of Riley's sorry ass! He's the one who deserves it!"

Keeping one arm circled around my waist, Adam follows behind Brad, who is making us a path through the crowd of people. I do notice that Brad is carrying my things from class in his hands so we don't have to stop and grab them.

The sun hits us as we breeze through the side entrance to the student parking lot. When we reach our vehicles, Adam turns to Brad. "What happened, man? Why weren't you with her?"

"Dude, I'm sorry. She got up and left the classroom about ten minutes before the bell rang. I got up to follow her, but Mr. Waterson wouldn't let me leave. I did keep my eye on Riley to make sure he didn't somehow sneak out or whatever," Brad explains regretfully.

"Why didn't you at least text me or something?"

"I couldn't send you a text because Mr. Waterson kept watching me."

"Adam, please, it's not his fault," I say, trying to defuse the situation.

Adam sighs and kisses my hair. "I know, I'm sorry. I'm just really pissed off right now." Adam turns back to Brad. "I'm sorry for the interrogation, man. I know it's not your fault," he says apologetically.

Brad slaps Adam's shoulder. "No problem, man, I understand."

I retrieve my things from Brad and say good-bye to him and Alexis. Adam opens the truck door for me and I climb in.

What happened earlier still bothers Adam, and I wish I knew what to say so I could fix it. I know he's worried about me, and I love him for it, but the situation could have been a lot worse.

Adam parks his truck in the driveway and climbs out. When he opens my door, I unbuckle my seatbelt, but I don't get out. With the way his jaw tenses, I know he is still pissed.

"Talk to me, Adam."

He shakes his head. "You need to go inside and lie down for a while, sweetheart, and rest."

"I'm not getting out of the truck until you talk to me."

He steps closer so he can caress my belly with his hands. "All three of you could have been seriously hurt, Kaylee."

I cup his face with my hands, wanting him to look me in the eye. "We are all fine, Adam," I say, trying to reassure him.

"That's not the point, sweetheart. One of them could have intentionally let you fall or someone could have hit or elbowed you in the stomach. I don't like seeing you hurt, but if something happens to one of my kids, I'll go crazy."

"And I love you for that, but remember what Dr. Lawson asked us to do? We need to just let this stay in the past and move on."

"I don't think this counts just yet."

"It's in the past, right? So, it counts."

Adam breathes in slowly and releases the breath. "Okay, it's going to take a good minute, but I will try and put it behind me."

"That's all I ask, babe."

## Alexis

*"Seeing Kaylee glow more and more as she progresses through her pregnancy is one of the most beautiful sights in the world."- Adam*

I am just putting the finishing touches on my make-up when I hear the doorbell ring. I fluff my hair and smooth out my shirt before going to let Brad inside. He didn't give me much information about our date; he just told me to be ready by five o'clock.

I open the door wide, meeting Brad's handsome face with a smile.

"Hey beautiful," he croons, holding out a bouquet of roses. I take them, admiring them, as I thank him. "You ready?"

"Yeah, let me put these in some water first."

I breeze into the kitchen, grab a vase, and fill it with water. These flowers are really beautiful. I set the vase with the roses in it on the kitchen table for now. I'll move them to my room when I get home tonight.

"Brad, where are we going?" I giggle as he leads me blindfolded to whatever surprise he has planned. I don't even know where we are. Brad had blindfolded me before I even got in his truck. I'm not complaining, though. While most people hate surprises, I love them.

His hands are on my shoulders, turning me in the direction we need to go. "You'll see soon enough."

"What's the surprise even for?"

"Just be patient and quit asking questions," he says.

I can hardly contain my excitement. I feel so bubbly and giddy that I would probably be skipping if Brad didn't have his hands on my shoulders.

We slow to a stop and my excitement grows tremendously. In my mind, I'm trying to think of what the surprise could be. I have no idea what the occasion is, but I guess I will find out soon.

Brad's hands slide down the lengths of my arms and slowly drift back up. I can feel him getting closer to me and hear his breathing pick up slightly. "Okay, now I'm going to let go of you. Do not take your blindfold off until I say so. Got it?" he murmurs in my ear.

"O-okay," I reply, sounding flustered from his close proximity.

Brad kisses my cheek and then his hands drop from my arms. I wait, rather impatiently, for him to instruct me to remove the black silk cover from my eyes.

"All right, Lex, you ready?" I swear I hear a hint of nervousness in his tone. Why would he be nervous?

"Yes!" I practically scream.

Brad chuckles and says, "I can tell."

I fold my arms across my chest, indicating my impatience. I'm really beyond impatient, but he doesn't need to know that.

Several long moments later, I hear him say the words I've been dying to hear. "You can remove the blindfold, Lex," he says softly.

My fingers grasp the material and tug at it, freeing my eyes. I drop the blindfold and let out an audible gasp, my hands flying to my mouth in shock. Before me, along the sidewalk, is an arrangement of red roses and candles. The candles spell out 'Prom?' I look around, finally noticing where I am. We are standing in the entrance Ledgewood Park, the park Brad took me to on our first date. We had a lovely picnic consisting of Chinese food. We sat for hours and talked, getting to know one another.

Brad stands off to the left of his beautiful creation with his hands stuffed in his pockets. He looks relaxed, though slightly nervous. Brad clears his throat and steps forward, holding out his hand for me. The sun casts an orange glow on his handsome face as it sets in the West. I place my hand in his, my stomach fluttering with anticipation of what he is going to say. "The girl standing before me is as beautiful as the sunset. The girl holding my hand right now holds my heart in the palm of her hand. The girl I'm in love with is carefree, headstrong, determined, and outgoing, and I'm hoping she will go to prom with me."

I stare at him, awestruck. Did he just say he was in love with me? Am I in love with him? Yes, I believe I am. I know I feel strongly for Ethan, but I'm tired of wasting my time wanting someone who doesn't want me in return.

The poem was cheesy good, if that is such a thing. Brad is amazingly sweet, too sweet. I had been thinking about prom over the last week, and while I kind of wanted Ethan to be my date, I knew it wouldn't happen. Besides, Brad just blew him out of the water with his prom proposal. I swear this boy is a born romantic.

"Uh, Lex, an answer would be nice right about now."

I cup the back of his neck and crush his mouth to mine. His tongue dances with mine seductively. We finally draw back for air and I ask, "How's that for an answer?"

His lips curl into a smile. "Best. Answer. Ever."

"Um, I think I heard you say that you love me. Is that true?"

His smile widens noticeably. "Yes, Lex, you heard me correctly. You are the first girl I've felt this strongly about. I love you, Alexis, and I hope you love me, too."

I leap into his arms, and he spins me around. My feet barely touch the sidewalk before I'm suddenly dipped and kissed like I've never been kissed before. I let out a small squeal and giggle, my lips brushing his. "You could have warned me that you were going to do that!"

"No, it would have just taken all the fun out of it."

He stands me back up but doesn't let me go.

"Do you really love me?" I murmur, wondering why he would be in love with me. Don't get me wrong, Brad and I are wonderful together, but having feelings for someone else that just won't go away can make me question everything.

He tucks a strand of hair behind my ear. "Yes, I do, Alexis. I wouldn't say it if I didn't mean it. You don't have to say it back. I'm just letting you know how I feel."

I honestly don't know what to say to him. Believing I'm in love with him feels like I'm second-guessing myself. I don't feel a hundred percent positive in love with him, and I'm definitely not going to say those three small, powerful words until I'm absolutely certain. I hope it doesn't hurt his feelings.

"Brad, I-"

He interrupts me by kissing me. "I can see the indifference in your eyes. You're unsure, and like I just said, I'm okay with it."

"You're too good to me," I murmur honestly because he is.

"No, I'm the lucky one here. I just asked this amazing girl to prom and she said yes."

My heart swells with so much emotion, I'm afraid it might burst. "I can't wait to go to prom with you, Brad. I hope it will be awesome."

"It will be awesome because I will be with you."

My face heats, flaming red.

Brad takes me to my favorite place to eat, Garcia's Mexican Restaurant. They have the best cheese dip and chicken fajitas.

We are in and out fairly quickly and are off to our final destination for the night, Cue Time Billiards.

I haven't played pool, well, since the last time Brad brought me here, which was a couple of weeks ago. Brad and I love coming here to hang out. They play some awesome music and the people here are friendly. I'm not great at this game, but with Brad's help, I'm getting better.

Brad leans forward to whisper in my ear. "You know, I'm going to enjoy watching you bend over the table."

I throw my head back and laugh. "Is that so? Well, I hope you like what you see."

"Oh, I know I will."

Something in the atmosphere shifts, leaving me bewildered. I feel eyes burning a hole the size of Texas onto me. It could only be one person. *Ethan.* I look over my shoulder, instantly spotting him several tables away. He must sense my gaze because his head snaps in my direction. He is standing with three other guys though none of them holds a candle to him. Ethan has his own category of hotness.

Brad hasn't spotted him yet, which is why he does the worst thing he could do to a girl in my position, and that is to leave me alone. Brad walks away to grab us some more drinks.

No sooner than Brad walks away, here comes one of Ethan's buddies.

"Hi, I'm Cole. You're Alexis, right?" Cole is nice looking for a guy with long hair and tattoos.

"That's me, the one and only," I reply coolly, offering my hand for him to shake.

"Pretty much the only reason I came over here is to make Ethan sweat."

I glance at Ethan to find him gripping the edge of the pool table with so much force I'm surprised he hasn't broken off a piece yet. "That's very kind of you," I reply, laughing at how forward he is.

"For real though, he has it bad for you. He about beat the shit out of me when I told him if he wouldn't go talk to you, then I would."

I know Ethan is attracted to me; I can see it, I feel it, when we are around each other. I wish he wouldn't hold back with me. I need him to be upfront with his feelings so I know I can trust him. I'm not interested in Ethan for a short period of time; I want him for the long haul. If he can't be open and honest about what he wants with me, how can I trust him?

"If he has it as bad as you say he does, then why is he not doing anything about it? I've tried, but he won't budge. I'm starting to think he'd rather have the comfort of a whiny bitch than me."

Cole's body rumbles with laughter. "That would be Kate, and you're right, she's definitely a bitch. None of us knows why he deals with her."

"Rejection hurts. I have Brad and he is amazing, but…" I drop my gaze to the floor; I'm embarrassed and pissed at myself for letting Ethan get to me again.

"But he isn't Ethan," Cole finishes for me.

I look up and shake my head. "No, he's not. I feel more fire, more spark, from just being around Ethan than I do from kissing Brad. That makes me sound awful, doesn't it?"

"No, it makes you human. From what I'm gathering, Brad is your safe choice."

I nod, letting him know he is right. Laughter bubbles up my throat. "I can't believe that I'm telling you all of this."

"My lips are sealed, pinky promise. Well, it was nice meeting you. Hopefully, we'll be meeting again soon." He surprises me by wrapping his arms around me, hugging me. "I know I'm going to catch hell for that, but you are just too sweet. I better go before your boyfriend comes back and decks me," he says with a laugh. "Chin up, girl. I bet he will give in to his feelings soon. If he doesn't, he's an idiot."

I smile genuinely at him. "Nice meeting you, too," I reply as he walks away.

I look over my shoulder and notice that Brad is making his way back. I force a smile and thank him when he hands me the water I asked for.

Let's hope Cole is right about Ethan. My heart can't take much more rejection from him.

*Ethan*

*"I haven't told Kaylee this, but I'm as scared as I am excited about being a father. I'm ready for this journey with her though."- Adam*

Finally, after searching for the last few months, I have a job. I, Ethan Harper, am now a police officer for the Bowling Green Police Department. Tonight, I'm celebrating with some friends I haven't seen in a while. Keith, Zack, and Cole are driving up and meeting me at Cue Time Cocktails and Billiards to shoot some pool and drink some beer. I'm in desperate need of a night out with the guys, who are some old high school buddies of mine. We've kept in touch over the years and have hung out many times, even while I was overseas. They all helped me deal with not only losing Dad, but Kaylee as well. I haven't talked to them since I moved up here to find my sister, so it's definitely time to catch up.

I walk into the building and head straight for the bar.

"What can I get for you?" the bartender asks.

"Bud Light." He nods and walks away to grab my drink.

"Harper!"

I turn around and see the guys walk up. We slap hands and greet one another. The bartender returns with my drink and takes their order.

"So, Harper, what's been happening? Did you find your sister?" Cole asks, starting the conversation. All four of us match in height and body size. Cole has shoulder length blond hair, a sleeve of tattoos, and blue eyes. Zack has curly, sandy blond hair, green eyes, and two skull tattoos, one on each shoulder. Keith has the preppy boy haircut; his hair is jet black, no tattoos, and green eyes. These guys are like my brothers, they always have my back.

*Oh, I found more than her.* "Yeah, I did."

"Well?" Zack presses.

"It's a long story, but it turns out that her mother played us both. Kaylee was told I didn't want to see her; she thought I blamed her for what happened to Dad."

Keith slaps my shoulder. "Well, shit man, that sucks."

"Yeah, but everything is good between us now."

Zack eyes me suspiciously. "I think you're holding out on us, man. What else has been going on?"

I sigh heavily, staring at the beer bottle in my hand. "Lots of things." They all stare at me, waiting for me to tell them, so I start with the first time I saw Kaylee. They all listen intently as I tell them everything that has happened over the last few months. When I get to the heavy part, I pause for a moment. It doesn't get easier hearing or repeating any of it. I try not to get caught up and washed away in the guilt, but the feeling is still there.

"Why didn't you call us, man? You know we would help you in any way we can," Cole replies. Keith and Zack nod in agreement.

"There is nothing anyone can do except wait and pray the judge gives him a life sentence." Not very likely to happen, but we all can hope.

"Or the death penalty would be a nice possibility," Keith mutters. Again, not likely, but we are hopeful for it, too.

I feel my phone vibrate in my pocket so I pull it out and check the screen. *Kate.* She is really starting to get on my nerves. She is becoming too clingy, always wanting to know where I am and who I am with, and it's becoming annoying. I hit ignore and pocket my phone.

"I know that look, girl problems, right?" Keith asks with a laugh.

I grunt in response and pull out my phone, which is vibrating again. I excuse myself from the guys so I can see what Kate needs. It had better be important. Kate and I are off and on all the time. More off than on, though, here lately with Alexis leaving me with blue balls, we have been seeing each other more than usual. I'm sure that's why she is ringing my phone off the hook now.

"Yeah," I bark out, irritated because she won't leave me alone.

"Ethan," she whines, and I cringe. Hearing her whine reminds me of the nails on a chalkboard sound. "Where are you?"

"I'm out with the guys." No need to inform her of where I am. Otherwise, I can guarantee that she will make a surprise visit.

"Oh, when will you be home?"

"Late. Bye, Kate." I hang up on her and head back to the bar. I need another drink after hearing her voice.

I order another drink and down half of it in two large swallows.

"Yeah, he is definitely having girl problems," Keith announces, proving he was right to begin with.

"Let's just hope it's not the girl we think it is," Cole adds with a groan.

He is partly right, except I am having problems with one they don't know about.

"Please tell us it's not Kate. I swear, man, I will choke you if you say Kate." This is from Zack, who between the four of us is the threatening one.

I shrug one shoulder. "Okay, it's not Kate."

Keith slaps the counter. "Liar!" he yells, gaining the attention of the people surrounding us.

"Let's go play some pool," I say, trying to deflect the conversation to something else. I know how they feel about her; they've made it known many times.

"Sure, we'll play, but we are still talking about this," Zack replies.

We leave the bar after ordering another round, making our way to the pool tables, which are in the other room. I make it three steps through the door before halting, her laughter crashing into me with so much force that I stumble slightly. I scan the room, looking for the source of the laughter.

The guys bump into me from behind with my sudden stop. "Dude, why'd you stop?"

I ignore Zack and continue with my scan of the perimeter. Bingo. My hands fist at my sides seeing her here with him. Brad has his hands on her waist, whispering something in her ear. She throws her head back and laughs again. It is a direct hit to my gut.

Cole whistles loudly. "Who is that beautiful creature?"

I look over my shoulder, glaring at him so hard he could melt into ashes. "Don't even think about it. Besides, she's taken anyway." The last part I say with sadness. Not to mention he is five years her senior, like me.

They all start firing off questions. Who is she? How do I know her? Who is the guy with her? I just tune them out and walk to the open pool table, which is on the other side of the room. I need to be as far away from her as possible so she can't suck me in. *Too late,* my subconscious screams.

Their questions return as Keith racks the balls.

Having heard enough, I throw my hands in the air in defeat. "Fine, her name is Alexis, and she is Kaylee's best friend. The guy with her is Brad, her boyfriend," I say the last part as a growl. My eyes search for her across the room. I spot her immediately; she is smiling at him, leaving me wishing she were smiling at me that way.

"She looks kind of young. How old is she?"

I knew they would catch on to how young and vibrant she looks. "Seventeen."

They all whistle low.

"She'll be eighteen in May."

"Wow, man, what else have you been holding out on?"

"That's it."

"Does she know you're interested?"

"Really, Cole? I just told you that she is with her boyfriend. But to answer your question, no. She's made it known how she feels, but I just pretend to be indifferent."

All three of them look at me like I have lost my ever-loving mind.

Zack grabs my chin, forcing me to look in her direction. If only he knew how hard it is to look at her and not walk over there and kiss her senseless. "Dude, look at her. How can you say no to that?"

I smack his hand away. "She is jail bait, you ass. Plus, she looks happy so I'm not going to ruin it." My eyes drift back to her like they don't want to look at anything else.

"What a pathetic excuse. Try again."

"I'm fixing to get shipped out in November, guys. Why promise her things when I may not be able to fulfill them?

"Are you listening to yourself? You'll come back, Ethan. I know you, and I know you don't go down without a fight."

"When you come back, we will have a six pack waiting on you," Keith adds with a laugh. We all laugh with him, but inside I'm dead silent. It is scary knowing I may not get to see my family or Lex again.

This time when I look back at her, she is already staring at me, her eyes wide. Neither one of us expected to see the other here. I stiffen when she bends over to take a shot; her ass is directly in my line of vision. She looks over her shoulder and winks at me. Are you kidding me? She thinks this is a game? I grip the pool stick in my hand so hard I could break it. I bring my beer to my lips and take a long swig.

"If you won't go talk to her, I will."

I grab Cole by the shirt and yank him forward. "Like hell you will."

He chuckles and I tighten my grip. "Bro, I was messing with you. You know me better than that."

With a curse, I release him. "Sorry man, she is driving me crazy. She taunts me all the time."

Cole slaps me on my shoulder. "Be right back, man." He takes off across the room to her, leaving me to curse after him. What in the hell is he doing?

I keep my eyes trained on him, making sure he doesn't get too close to her and not one finger touches her. I grip the edge of the pool table so hard my knuckles turn stark white. I search the crowd for Brad, but I can't find him.

Cole has always been the brazen one. He isn't afraid to do anything, it doesn't matter how embarrassing it could be.

Alexis watches him cautiously, her eyes drifting over to me every now and then. She obviously doesn't know what to think of him. I can see her slowly let her guard down after a minute or two. What is he saying to her? Lord knows it is probably something I wouldn't approve of. Hell, he could be telling her that I'm suffering over here without her. Knowing Cole, he is more than likely telling her I'm hiding how I feel from her. The outcome could be good or bad. I'm guessing bad since she already tries to break me. Now, she will only try harder, and I don't know how much longer I can restrain from kissing those red, plump lips. A man can only take so much, and with a goddess like her, he will give in easily.

A growl releases from my throat when I see Cole hug her. He and I are going to have words. Cole is now walking back with a shit-eatin' grin plastered on his face. I don't dare look her way again. God, I should get a freakin' medal for fighting this hard to keep my distance. She doesn't make it easy, that's for sure. Alexis knows what in the hell she is doing.

And what's worse is I don't want her to quit because then it will mean she has given up on me. It will mean she doesn't want me anymore. How long would she wait for me? How long will she stay with him even though I know I'm the one she wants?

Cole is back and is currently laughing at me.

"What did you say to her?"

"Oh, nothing," he answers laughingly.

"Cole," I growl in warning.

He chuckles and places his hand on my shoulder. "We just had a little chat, Ethan. I wanted to get to know the girl that has Ethan Harper on his knees. Although, I did find out her exact feelings toward you."

"And?" I prompt him to continue.

"I guess the only way to find out is to get your ass in gear and prove to her how much you want her."

Damn him. I knew he wouldn't make this easy for me. He knows how much I like a challenge. Kaylee and I are alike in this way. We don't like things handed to us, we want to work for them.

Cole is testing me, and he knows that I will take the bait.

I want to tell Lex how I feel, but I'm afraid I'll get my heart broken in the process.

## Adam

*"I want to destroy the monster I created, but I think I'm too late. It has taken over my body, keeping me from changing back to the guy I was trying to be."- Riley*

Kaylee is shaking like a leaf in my arms as we wait for our lawyer to announce it's time. She is so nervous and scared to go out there. Hell, I'm nervous for her. She is going to have to get up in front of the courtroom and describe in detail all the pain she endured. Who wouldn't be scared to do that?

I kiss her temple and whisper soothing thoughts in her ear, hoping to ease her apprehension. Mom, Dad, Ethan, Brad, and Alexis are all here to support her as well. The outcome had better be in our favor today. Otherwise, I will be murderous. Riley shouldn't get a chance to take the stand and try to weasel his way out of going to jail. I hate this. I have a gut feeling this isn't going to go well.

The door opens to my right and Mr. Allison strolls in with a smile. We shake hands and make introductions.

He explains once again about what to expect. "Do any of you have any questions before we go in?" Mr. Allison looks at all us before lingering his gaze on Kaylee, who shakes her head. Mr. Allison checks his watch and informs us that it's time to go.

I let everyone else walk out ahead of us so I can have a moment alone with Kaylee. When they are all gone, I turn to her and cup her face in my hands. Her eyes are wet with tears. I thumb away the wetness on her cheeks and gaze deep into her frightened eyes.

"When you're up there, just keep your eyes on me. Don't worry about anyone else in the room. Just focus on me, okay? No matter what happens, remember that I love you." She nods slowly and I give her a chaste kiss as I drop my hand, threading our fingers together.

We walk quickly to catch up with the others. They are all standing outside the door to the courtroom, waiting for us.

I don't let go of Kaylee's hand until the last second. I take my seat on the bench right behind her chair. I look to my right at Riley's parents and notice they are glaring at Kaylee. I look at Riley's seat and notice that it is empty. Where is he?

We stand when the judge walks in and then sit back down when he motions for us to.

He didn't show up. His newly appointed lawyer, the reason for the delayed trial in the first place, hasn't heard from him. So now, the judge postponed the trial another two weeks. What game is he playing? What is he up to?

I wrap my arm around Kaylee's waist and lead her to my truck. She hasn't said a word, but I bet I know all the questions that are running through her mind this instant.

She half hugs everyone before climbing into my truck and shutting the door. I feel so bad for her. I wish there was something I could say or do to take her mind off the craziness for a while. All of this just needs to be over with so she can look into the future with a smile.

When I'm in, I lift the center armrest so she can sit next to me. I need to feel her against me so I can hold her and silently communicate that things will be okay. Truthfully, at this point, I'm not sure what to think. I, along with the others, thought that the trial would be long over, and if they made the right decision, Riley would be behind bars.

The ride home is quiet as Kaylee is staring out the windshield. Her hands rest on her stomach like she is comforting them.

This morning wasted our time. I have the urge to drive to him and drag his good for nothing ass to the judge. There is a warrant out for his arrest now, but it doesn't do any good if you can't find him. He has to be up to something. Why else would he skip the trial?

I need to cheer her up somehow. We both need to forget it all for a few days and just focus on us, our relationship. A light bulb flipped on in my head and I grin to myself. I know just what to do, especially since her birthday is next week.

I wait until Kaylee has laid down before texting Alexis and asking for help. She had better keep my plans a secret or I will be pissed. This pregnancy is exhausting Kaylee, and all the drama swirling around isn't helping. She needs to be relaxing, not worrying about Elizabeth and Riley.

This weekend can't get here fast enough. She is going to be mad since she hates surprises, but I hope once we get there, she will forget why she was mad in the first place.

In three days, I will have my girl all to myself for two days. Nothing can top what I'm feeling right now.

### Kaylee

I see two duffel bags sitting by the door with a smiling Adam not far away. My eyes dart between Adam and the bags suspiciously. "Do I even need to ask?" He is up to something, judging by the look in his eyes.

"You'll see soon enough."

Ugh! I hate surprises! My eyes narrow at him and he chuckles. "It's your birthday surprise." He bends down to give me a quick kiss before grabbing the bags.

"My birthday is not for another…" I ponder when it actually is. The last few months have been crazy so I guess it slipped my mind. "…right. Okay, so where are we going?"

He shakes his head. "Nope." He runs his fingers across his lips signaling they are sealed.

"Can you at least tell me where it is or what we will be doing?"

"What part of surprise don't you understand?" I roll my eyes at him and say my good-byes. Alexis gives me a wink. Bitch, she is also up to something. Either that or she knows exactly what's going on. I'm more afraid of her surprises than Adam's though. I have a feeling she packed my bag, and that thought alone frightens me. Or does it excite me?

Soon we were on our way through the city heading to who knows where. I have no idea how long it will take, either. I just stare out the window watching all the lights, cars, and the rest of my surroundings go by. It suddenly dawns on me that Adam and I haven't talked about our future. I don't know if he plans to go away to college or what. I knew I had planned to go away, but things have drastically changed since then. "What are your plans after graduation? What did you want to do?" I hold my breath waiting for his answer.

He grasps my hand letting his thumb stroke the back of my hand. "I decided I wanted to help Dad in the shop. Maybe someday I might take it over, who knows? Dad isn't pressuring me; he told me I could do anything I wanted, but I love being there, working on cars. As for school, I doubt I will go since I pretty much know everything about cars." I exhaled a sigh of relief. I'm happy that Adam and his dad get along so well. I've seen Adam come home a few times all greasy and he looked just as hot if not hotter than he usually does. "What are your plans?"

"Well, I honestly don't know. I haven't put much thought into it. I mean, at first I had planned to get away and prayed that I got a scholarship somewhere. Alexis and I had planned to apply to the same colleges so we didn't have to split up." I peek at him out of the corner of my eye. He is relaxed while concentrating on the road. His expression is unreadable. "Now, I'd rather focus on providing a life for thing one and thing two here. College doesn't appeal to me anymore. I just want to get a job so I can actually start having my own money and so I can help provide for all of us." I place my hand on my stomach while Adam chuckles at my nicknames for them.

"You have plenty of time to figure out what you want to do after the babies are born. I prefer you not to work and be a stay-at-home mom, though." I'm relieved to know that Adam's original plan wasn't to leave after graduation. It's amazing how when you least expect it life changes course and gets you on track to where you need to be. My life strayed from the path for years, but now it's finally back on the course.

"Can it be you who stays home while I work? I really want to get a job. Please? Look at it from my point of view, Adam. My whole life things have been handed to me from either my father or Alexis and now you and your family as well. I want the chance to actually take care of myself along with you and our kids." He sighs like he is considering my offer. I know this going to be a tough decision for him to make since he wants to provide for us. I love him for that, but I feel like I need to take charge of my life and stop mooching off people.

"We'll talk about it when the time comes. Right now, let's just enjoy our time together. You may change your mind once these little guys finally arrive." He lets go of my hand to rub my belly. My heart swells with emotion at how excited he is about these two little miracles. He lifts up the middle console and motions for me to lay down. I happily stretch out, resting my head on his leg. His fingers caress my cheek for a few minutes before finally doing the same with my belly. I'll love whatever the surprise is because I'm with the most handsome, sweetest man there is.

No doubt this weekend will be amazing.

## Adam

*"My future is always right next to me, holding my hand firmly in his grasp."- Kaylee*

After driving for two hours, I smile when I pull into my destination. She is going to love it. Kaylee finally gave in to sleep thirty minutes ago. She had been fighting to stay awake until we arrived, but she lost the battle and her eyes fluttered closed.

I look down at my sleeping beauty, feeling all kinds of emotion tugging at my heart. "Wake up, sweetheart. We're here," I murmur tenderly. Her eyes blink open a couple of times before she slowly sits up. She rubs her eyes with the heels of her hands before looking around and letting out a gasp. The lights twinkle in her eyes as she continues to be in awe of everything. The look on her face is better than I imagined it would be. "You want to see the rest of it?" She simply nods, still star struck. I climb out and grab our bags from the backseat. Holding the bags in one hand, I slide my hand into hers and bring it up to plant a kiss on the back of her hand before we make our way down the lighted trail. White lights with gardens of flowers on both sides glow along the trail that leads to the cabin I rented for two days. I will have her all to myself for two freakin' days.

I open the cabin door for her, tossing the bags on the floor. The cabin was decorated in rustic and vintage décor with hardwood floors. It had a full kitchen connected with the den. I step back, letting her roam the place. I follow her into the master bedroom that contains a king-size four-poster bed with rose petals scattered over it. I laugh when her mouth falls open at the sight of it. We make our way to the adjoined bathroom, and her eyes immediately fall to the large tub in the corner.

Kaylee slowly spins so we are eye to eye. "This is…amazing…breathtaking…thank you!" she exclaims, throwing her arms around my neck. I know I will have to top this when we go on our honeymoon, but I'm sure I could pull it off. That is if she agrees to marry me when I ask her. Marriage freaks most guys out, but not me. I know I have found the one girl I will love for eternity, and the idea of me getting to wake up to her gorgeous face every morning and every night before I close my eyes is…well, there are no correct words to describe how wonderful and amazing it would feel. No word I come up with seems enough.

"You're welcome, sweetheart. I wanted to do something special for you to show you how much I love you."

"Just being with you is enough. This… is too much." She waves her hands around, gesturing to the cabin. I cradle her face in my palms and kiss her hungrily. My mouth greedily finds hers over and over. She lets out the sweetest little moan setting my body on fire. All of my senses come alive when she runs her hands under my shirt, exploring my chest.

I plan to show her how much I love her over the next two days. We need this time together, just her and I. Life has been getting in our way, trying to knock us around. Thankfully, we haven't let go of each other through the hardships. If anything, we are stronger together.

Kaylee is my wildest dream come true in every imaginable way possible. I can't imagine my life or my future without her.

She grasps the hem of my shirt; her fingers graze my skin all the way up as she removes my shirt. I break away for a second to remove her t-shirt then my mouth is back on hers, tasting her. I feel like a starved man who can't get enough.

My hands cup her backside, lifting her. Her legs latch around my waist, her hands grip my biceps, as I walk us over to the bed, gently laying her across it. I kiss her rounded belly twice, once on each side. I discard her pants and mine on the floor with our shirts. I let my mouth explore every inch of her delectable body, torturing us both.

I make love to her, slowly, worshiping her until we both come undone. Our heavy breathing fills the room, our eyes transfixed on each other. She smiles up at me, her eyes telling me all the things she cannot say. I roll us over so she is lying on top of me. I kiss her forehead and tighten my arms around her.

We are quiet for a few passing moments, just enjoying being in each other's arms. Her stomach growls, interrupting the comforting silence, and we both laugh.

"How about I fix us something to eat? I'm sure thing one and thing two need to be fed," I smirk at her, mocking her nicknames for them.

"Hmm…that's my second favorite thing. I'm going to take a bath while you do that."

Wait, I thought food was her favorite thing? "Since food obviously has been downgraded, what is your favorite thing now?" I raise my brow at her in question. I catch a glimpse of her cheeks flushing before she covers her face, making me chuckle. "Don't get all shy on me now, sweetheart."

"You." One word. One. That's all it takes to start a frenzy of kisses.

I think the food will have to wait just a little bit longer.

*Kaylee*

While Adam orders dinner, I take a relaxing bubble bath in the giant tub I fell in love with earlier. This place is so beautiful. Maybe tomorrow we can go exploring.

I dig through my bag trying to find something to wear tonight. Oh, no. She did not…I'm going to kill Alexis! I grab my phone off the counter and dial her number. My foot taps impatiently as I wait for her to answer. She doesn't greet me; oh no, she laughs because she knows why I'm calling. Bitch.

"What the hell, Alexis! I can't wear this!" I examine the skimpy black material on top of my bag. She bought me lingerie. At least it's not pink.

"Yes, you can! Adam will love it!" I stick my head out the door making sure he is still in the kitchen. I put my phone on speaker and lay it on the counter. It doesn't hurt to try it on real quick. "Besides, he needs to see all the goods!" Oh, he has seen everything, a few times.

"He has already seen the whole package."

"Hold up! You two finally did the deed and I'm just now finding out?"

"This isn't the first time we have," I say, cringing with the realization that I haven't told her yet.

"Whoa, wait a second! You and Adam had sex and you didn't tell me?"

"It's not like I didn't want to; things have been so hectic lately, I forgot."

"Well, out with it, baby girl! I want details!"

I hurriedly tell her about our first time, not going into detail too much, while I finish putting on the outfit she secretly stuck in my suitcase.

"I don't have the body for this!" I fuss while snapping the top together. The only part not see-through is the bra section. The lace material that hangs from beneath it parts in the middle. It actually didn't look that bad.

"You tried it on, didn't you?" she asks with a laugh.

"Fine, yes, I did, but it's not staying on. Why didn't you pack normal clothes for me to sleep in?"

"Hot damn…please…for the love of God, leave it on." I spin around to see Adam standing in the doorway with his mouth hanging open. Alexis must have heard his comment because she is now rolling with laughter.

"What did I tell you, baby girl? Told you he'd love it!" I couldn't reply and neither could he. We are both frozen in place, our eyes locked on one another. He is clad only his boxers which made it hard for my eyes to just focus on one spot on his body. My mouth suddenly feels parched from the way he is looking at me. Our intense stare down finally relinquishes when he takes the first step, closing the gap between us. Alexis is rambling on about something. He leans over, without taking his eyes off me, and presses end, hanging up on her.

"You need to eat quickly before I lose the little bit of control I have left." *Oh, my*. How does he expect me to eat now with my stomach in knots? I lean in to kiss him, but he steps away. "If you kiss me, I damn sure will not be able to stop."

Begrudgingly, I leave on the outfit and sashay past him. Really, I forgot all about having it on.

"Kaylee," he growls in warning. I grin to myself and keep walking as if I didn't hear him.

Adam sits across from me, watching me eat. He has already cleaned his plate. I am taking my sweet time, savoring my food. Mainly so I can enjoy sitting here watching him squirm.

"Can you eat a little faster?" he asks breathlessly.

I keep my expression cool, not wanting him to know I'm doing this on purpose. "Just be patient, I'm almost done."

"It's kind of hard to be patient when you are sitting close to me wearing that."

I reach across the bar, placing my hand on top of his. The smile I thought I had suppressed breaks free. I am trying to think of something to say, but I come up short. "Yeah, I got nothing."

He withdraws his hand from under mine and stands. He grabs my plate and takes the fork from my hand. "Hey! I was eating that!"

He throws the plate in the trash and the fork in the sink. "No, you weren't. You were just toying with me."

"It was kind of fun," I tease.

"You want fun? I'll show you fun." He sweeps me in his arms, carrying me bridal style back to the bedroom.

I giggle when he drops me on the bed and climbs on top of me.

I start squirming when he finds my ticklish spots. "Adam…please…stop!" I get out between laughter.

He finally relinquishes and I catch my breath.

I freeze when I feel movement in my stomach. "Adam," I murmur in awe. I grab his hand, placing it on my belly where I felt them moving. "Feel this."

"Wow," he whispers in amazement. Adoration is all over his face.

"You woke them up," I say with a laugh.

Adam leans in close to my stomach. "Hey, you two. It's about time you woke up." He stretches out on the bed, propping his face on the heel of his hand. His free hand rests on my stomach.

And that is how the rest of the night is spent. Adam alternates between having a conversation with the twins and me. Occasionally, he will kiss my stomach and tell them how much he loves them. My love for Adam grows every day. He always does something that makes me love him more.

Reality bites. Darn you, reality! Why do we have to return so soon? This getaway has been amazing, relaxing, and very much needed. Adam and I ventured out and explored the area yesterday, finding this place to be more beautiful than I originally thought. A trail led back to a lake with a stone bridge leading to a gazebo. We visited the gazebo more than once. We talked, danced, kissed, and laughed for hours. I never wanted to leave, but our days were up. The whole ride home, I sat next to Adam, resting my head on his shoulder and replaying the last couple of days. As we walk up to the front door, I can't shake the nervousness. I don't know if I can look at Anna and Jack now without being embarrassed. I'm sure they know what we were up to. I just hope they don't make us sleep separately now. I'd be tossing and turning all night without Adam in bed with me.

"SURPRISE!" everyone yells, making me jump closer to Adam. Pink streamers and balloons decorate the house. On the kitchen table sits a cake and presents.

I glare at Adam. "I thought we discussed we wouldn't celebrate my birthday?"

He chuckles. "I agreed. They didn't." He had me there. "Happy birthday, sweetheart." He leans down and kisses me.

"My birthday is not until tomorrow," I say matter-of-factly.

He shrugs his shoulders. "So? I wanted to be the first one to tell you."

I was about to answer him when Alexis pretty much attacks me. "Happy birthday, baby girl!"

She lets go of me and Ethan swoops in. "Happy birthday, sis! It's about time you became an adult." I laugh and push him.

Anna and Jack are waiting behind him. "Happy birthday, sweetie." She steps back and lets Jack get a hug. "Happy birthday, Kaylee."

God, I love this family so much. "Thank you, but you shouldn't have gone to all this trouble for me!" They all shrug as if it is no big deal. Dad used to make a big deal over my birthday. He would go overboard with decorations, presents, games, food…you name it, he did it. Elizabeth would just roll her eyes and say we didn't need all of this and that it was too extravagant though she was the one to talk. She liked her rings shiny and her cars flashy. She didn't think I deserved a thing, thus why she protested about my prodigal birthday parties. I would have been happy with keeping things simple, though. However, Dad thought I deserved the "best." I'm glad that I didn't turn out to be one of those spoiled brat rich kids. No doubt Elizabeth thought I was one, but I never demanded something from Dad. I would ask occasionally for something though it was nothing over the top, just simple.

Alexis snapping her fingers in front of me brings me back from my daze. "Where'd you go?"

"I was thinking about the last time I had a birthday party. Dad was always overdoing it. He had rented a big community center and a few of the inflatable bouncy things, decorations were everywhere, and my cake was a three-tier princess theme. I even had a white horse and carriage that we all took turns riding. Dad had dressed up as a prince since we all had costumes." I giggle at the thought of Dad dressing up. "Ironically, Elizabeth was the evil witch." I roll my eyes dramatically. "It was by far the best party a twelve-year-old could ask for." My thirteenth birthday was the worst. Not having my father with me was hard.

I don't realize I am just rambling until I look up at everyone. Anna and Alexis are misty eyed while Jack and Ethan are smiling sympathetically. Adam slides his hand in mine, linking our fingers. I don't have to look at him to know what he is thinking; by grabbing my hand, he said it all. This is my family now. I hadn't had one in so long, I forget how good it feels to have people who care about you and love you like their own.

## Kaylee

*"Every day that passes, I find myself missing my father more and more. The guilt is finally gone, but my heart still hurts."- Kaylee*

"That one!" I squeal, pointing at the candy apple red Ford Edge. We are at our local Ford dealer so I can pick out a car. When Adam woke me up this morning, I grumbled for him to leave me alone, but when he reminded me where we were going, I was up faster than I ever have been before.

I can't believe that I'm finally getting a car! This is starting out to be the best birthday I've had in a long time. I picked the Edge because I wanted something other than a car for the babies, but I didn't want a van or a Tahoe. Those are too big. Not to mention this one is a gorgeous car! The interior was all black with leather seats. It even had a sunroof! I couldn't wait to drive it again. Adam rode with me while I took it for a test drive, and I instantly fell in love with it. When I asked Adam if he liked it, he said that it was my decision and I needed to get the one I wanted though he did like it.

A couple of hours later, I am heading to meet Alexis for lunch before we go shopping. Adam went to meet up with Ethan at their normal hangout. It feels prodigious to be able to buy something with my own money. I've longed to be able to do this. Though I wish I had earned the money, at least I didn't have to borrow money from anyone again. Although I was way out of my budget, I felt like I needed something reliable. The salesman was shocked when I came back with the full amount for the car.

"Look at you, hot mama!" Alexis met me outside the restaurant so she could see my new car. "I'm so jealous now! I think I might get me one!" she teases.

"Well, since I'm fixing to pay you back for all that I owe you, you can."

She automatically shakes her head. "Baby girl, you don't owe me a penny."

Oh, no. I'm definitely going to pay her back. "The only reason I accepted those gifts was because you agreed to let me pay you back."

"Exactly, they were gifts. I only said that so you would accept them."

"Fine," I huff knowing this conversation wouldn't go anywhere. "Since you won't let me pay you back, will you at least let me buy you lunch?"

"Sure, I'm down with that!" She links her arm with mine as we walk inside.

Alexis and I catch up on girl talk. She grilled me with questions about my romantic getaway with Adam. My face was scorching when I finished filling her in on the details. I tried to keep hushed so the people around us couldn't hear. It was embarrassing enough telling my best friend.

"Oh, guess what!" Alexis looks like she is about to jump out of her seat. "Brad asked me to prom!" Wow...I wasn't expecting that.

"What did you tell him?" I tried to sound happy for her. I am, but I was just hoping her and my brother would get together.

"Yes, silly! Duh!"

"That's great! I'm happy for you!" I am, really. As long as she is happy, I am.

I wonder if Ethan has given any thought to pursuing Alexis since our talk. I can tell they are both interested in each other so why are they fighting it? It occurred to me that Alexis still might be leaving after graduation. I'd hate not to be able to see my best friend, but if leaving makes her happy, then I'll deal with it.

"I know you had mentioned going away for college. Is that what you're doing?"

"Actually, no, I've changed my mind. Did you really think I'd leave my best friend and my nieces or nephews behind?" I let out a sigh of relief though I feel kind of guilty that she is only staying behind for me.

"You don't have to stay behind for me. If going away is what you really want, you need to do it."

"The only reason I had planned on moving was so I could get you far away from that evil bitch. Besides, I'm staying here for other reasons, too." Bingo. She doesn't want to move away from my brother.

I raise my brow at her pryingly. "Would Ethan happen to be one of them?"

She looks down at her food, trying to hide her smile. It disappeared as quickly as it appeared. "He is so confusing. One minute he acts like he wants me and then the next, he acts like I'm his sister's best friend." She sighs, playing with her food. "I know he is five years older, but it doesn't matter to me. I wish I knew how he really felt."

I was about to answer her when my phone chimed with a message. My eyes widen when I read the text from my mother.

**Mother:** *Come get your shit before I toss it out the damn window!*

It's not like I have been living there for the past few months, so why now, of all days, is she suddenly wanting me to come get my things?

"Is everything okay?" Alexis' voice registers in my brain. I totally forgot about her sitting there.

"I'm sorry, but I have to go. Mom is threatening to toss my stuff out of the window." I give her a weak smile before getting up and paying for our food.

"I will go with you. I don't want you going into that dungeon alone."

I turn onto the highway and follow behind Alexis, heading to Mom's. I did not want to spend my birthday in my old bedroom with Mom breathing down my neck. A shiver creeps its way up my spine thinking about the last time I was in there.

*I need to call Adam.* I pick up my phone out of the cup holder and hastily try to dial his number. I stop before I press the last number and glance in my rearview mirror. I gasp in horror and drop my phone. I blink my eyes several times, hoping and praying the car behind me is only my imagination. I grip the steering wheel in my hands and take a deep breath, trying to calm the nerves that have swarmed my body.

Riley's Mustang is two car lengths behind me. At first, I just thought it was a car similar to his until I saw his face. His cold stare meets mine in the mirror and I force my gaze to stay locked on Alexis' car in front of me. It may be just a coincidence that he happens to be behind me…going the same direction as me. Dang it, I wish I could reach my phone.

I take one last look in the mirror as I turn on Mom's street and release a breath when he keeps going.

I pull in my mother's driveway behind Alexis and sigh heavily as I get out. I don't want to be here nor do I want to see my so-called mother. The mother who betrayed me, who hates me.

Alexis walks over to me and eyes me suspiciously. "Everything okay, baby girl?" I love and hate that she can tell when something's amiss.

"Riley was following me."

Her eyes bug out. "What?!" she screeches. "Why didn't you call me?"

"I wanted to, but I dropped my phone and I couldn't reach it," I explain. "Anyway, when we turned, he kept going."

She throws her arm around me, ushering me inside. "Come on, let's get this over with. I'm going to text Brad so they know where we are." She pulls out her phone, sends Brad a text, and deposits her phone back in her pocket.

Mom is standing at the top of the stairs with her arms crossed, scowling at us when we walk in. "It's about time you got here," she sneers. "Good grief, Kaylee, you look huge!"

I ignore her rude comment and begin my trek up the stairs. I'm wearing the biggest shirt I own and my bump is still showing. I have one week left until I find out the gender and I can't wait to see them again. It will also be the first time Adam gets to see them on the ultrasound so I know it will be bittersweet.

"Hurry up and get out." With that, she turns and heads for her office.

Alexis and I roll our eyes and walk into my old room. My skin crawls at the memories. Everything seems to be untouched, except for the bed. I wonder when she made it?

I start with my desk while Alexis heads straight for my closet. Of course, the closet would be where she starts. I don't want everything. I just want the important stuff like pictures of Dad and me, things that Dad bought me over time that I kept, and a few other belongings. I bet money that Alexis will pack my whole closet, seeing how clothes and shoes are what she deems important.

We are halfway through packing up my stuff when Mom saunters in the room. She leans against the doorjamb wearing a snooty expression. I wish she would just stay locked in her office until I leave. "I can't wait for the trial next week. I'm going enjoy watching them tear you apart," she gloats, and I try to ignore her. "Haven't you wondered why they couldn't find any evidence? How he has been getting out on bail?" I tense, not knowing where she is going with this. "It's a pretty great story. Do you want to hear it? Of course, you do. You see, I was here that glorious night and I have to say, he did well. He was sloppy though, so I knew I had work to do. As soon as Adam took you away, I made quick work of washing the sheets and disinfecting anything Riley could have touched. I couldn't let him go to jail over something I thought you deserved."

My blood runs cold at her words. Did she really just admit to covering up the evidence? I hear Alexis gasp and drop whatever she had in her hands. Alexis turns and unleashes on her. "You bitch! How could you do that to your daughter? Your own flesh and blood?"

She thrusts her perfectly manicured finger toward me. "She took my husband from me! Jason and I loved each other. Everything was perfect until she came along and took all of his time, all of his love, and even all of his money. I hated you the moment I found out I was pregnant because I knew you would change things and you did. I told him that I wanted an abortion, but no, he wanted you and threatened to leave me if I went through with it." Venom drips like rain from her hateful words. I already knew Mom hated me, but her words still slice open the old wound I thought I had sewn together. She reaches behind her and draws a gun. Alexis is immediately at my side, squeezing my hand.

Alexis' phone starts ringing from her back pocket.

"Don't you dare answer it!" Elizabeth threatens. It stops and starts ringing again. "Hand it to me!" Alexis obeys her command, handing it over. Elizabeth takes our only form of communication and chunks it at the wall. It hits the beige colored wall with a loud thud and lands on the carpet. The back and the battery break apart from it.

Alexis grips my hand so hard I believe she will crush it, but I'm so numb I can't even feel the pain. The woman who gave birth to me is pointing a gun at me like she doesn't have a care in the world. "Why are you doing this?" I ask, trying to stall her. If I know the guys, they are probably on their way here since we haven't answered.

She laughs haughtily. "Why? Jason left me nothing! I'm his wife; I should get everything!"

"Why did you tell Ethan that I didn't want to see him? I needed my brother!"

"Because I wanted you to pay the price for killing my husband. I wanted you to feel broken and alone. You needed to know what it felt like to have the person you loved the most ripped away from you!"

"The night my father died was the night I lost the person I loved the most! He was my father, my best friend! So I knew already how it felt!"

"It wasn't enough for me. I wanted revenge. If you two weren't so close, you wouldn't have gone out that night, and he would still be here!"

"He was dying!"

She blanches. "What on Earth are you talking about?"

"Dad left me a letter explaining that he had cancer and he was dying. There was nothing the doctors could do," I explain.

"You're lying! He would have told me!"

I throw my hands in the air, giving up. I know I won't win with her. She will believe what she wants. "Whatever, Elizabeth."

She flips the safety off and steadies her aim, pointing the gun at me. "I should have done this a long time ago."

I murmur up a quick prayer for all of us, wishing there was some way I could stall her. I thought the guys would be here by now.

Alexis trembles in fear next to me. "Kaylee."

A gut wrenching sob erupts from my throat as I realize this is it.

The gun suddenly goes off and a black blur clouds my line of vision. "Alexis, no!" But it's too late. The bullet strikes her and she lands on the carpeted floor with a thud. I drop to my knees to aid my best friend. Through blurred vision, I blindly search for the wound. "ALEXIS!" I scream until my voice breaks.

I snap my head up to her when I hear her laugh wickedly. "Tell your father I love him for me."

*Adam*

*"I had to try and save her. I couldn't go on with my life knowing all of this was my fault."-Riley*

Ethan, Brad, and I are all lounging around my house waiting on the girls to get done. We are all going out to eat tonight for Kaylee's birthday as soon as they get here. Surprisingly, Brad and Ethan have been getting along today, even though they have their reservations with one another since they both want the same girl. Maybe they have finally figured out their shit. One can only hope.

A frantic knock has all of us looking at each other with curiosity. Who could that be?

We all three get up and walk to the front door where the frantic knocking continues.

I swing the door open, ready to face whoever the punk is, and my blood instantly starts simmering. Riley is the last person I expected to be on the other side.

His eyes are wide with panic. "You guys have to get to Elizabeth's now! Kaylee and Alexis are in danger!"

I look over at Ethan and Brad. All three of us burst out laughing at once. I don't know what crap he is trying to pull, but I'm not going to fall for it. He is a damn good actor, though; I'll give him that. If I didn't know him or if he hadn't hurt Kaylee, I'd actually believe him.

"Dude, we are not falling for it. We know where the girls are at and it isn't at Elizabeth's."

"Yes, they are! I was behind them! I watched them turn down the street!"

My fists connect with his face, and he stumbles backward. I march over to him and grab him by his shirt. "I don't want to see or hear of you following her anymore, got me?"

"It's not for the reasons that you think."

"Fine, I'll play. Why have you been following her?"

"I messed up, all right! To make a long story short, I made the stupidest decision of my life. I was in deep and Elizabeth offered a way out so I took it. Once the deal was made, I found out what she really wanted me to do. It gutted me to hurt Kaylee, but I didn't have a choice!" he rushes out, hardly taking a breath.

"You always have a choice, Riley! You should have taken the consequences instead of beating her and stripping her of her innocence!"

"I am a coward! I chickened out every time! Elizabeth took it too far and now the girls are over there in danger."

"What makes you say that?!"

"Elizabeth has something up her sleeve, though I'm not sure what it is. I have been postponing the trial so I can take her down with me. I needed evidence and I couldn't do it with her watching my every move. Once I turned eighteen three weeks ago, I paid off what I owed her, so I'm out."

I can't believe what I'm hearing. I unlatch my hands from his shirt and stand up straight. I pull out my phone and call Kaylee, praying that she answers. My heart beats rapidly every second I wait for her to pick up, but she never does. Why didn't she let me know she was going there?

Out of the corner of my eye, I see Brad checking his phone. "Uh, Adam. Alexis texted me about twenty minutes ago saying they are at Elizabeth's."

"Shit," I curse and run to my truck. Brad and Ethan are right behind me, one climbing in the front and the other climbing in the back. Thankfully, no one parked behind me so I can get out.

I send up a silent prayer that Riley is wrong about them being in danger.

"I'm calling 911, just in case," Ethan announces from the passenger seat. I'm glad he thought of that because I didn't. Maybe we won't need them. Riley could be overreacting about this, although I don't want to take any chances where Kaylee is concerned. Not with her or our babies in possible danger. I can't lose either of them. They are my life; my world revolves around them.

I screech to a stop at the edge of the driveway and leap out of my truck.

Sure enough, I see Kaylee's brand new car and Alexis' Altima parked in Elizabeth's driveway. The second my hand grabs the doorknob, my worst nightmare comes to life. The sound of a gunshot rings through my ears.

My blood runs cold when a horrifying scream erupts from the house. "Kaylee!" I yell as I burst through the door. I'm afraid of what I will see when I run in. I skid to a stop when I run in her room. Elizabeth towers over Kaylee, who is on her knees, sobbing over Alexis, pointing the gun at her face.

Ethan runs around me, heading straight for Elizabeth and tackling her to the ground. The gun clatters to the floor, out of her reach, so Brad and I run over to the girls. I pull Kaylee in my arms, holding her trembling body against me. The reality of what just happened hits me with full force. Riley, the guy I hate for what he did to Kaylee, just saved her life. If he hadn't warned us, I would have lost her. I wouldn't have known to come save her.

Brad yanks his shirt off, applying pressure to the bleeding wound on Alexis' stomach.

Ethan is suddenly between us, on his phone, talking to the dispatcher. "Seventeen-year-old female, gunshot wound to her abdomen. She is unresponsive…" I tune him out after that, switching my focus back to my girl in my arms.

I look to my left at Elizabeth, who is clutching her arm, whimpering in pain. Serves her right. I look around searching for the gun, making sure she can't get it, but I can't find it. I snap my head over to Ethan. "Where's the gun?" He responds by patting his shirt, letting me know that he has it.

The EMTs rush in minutes later to attend to Alexis. One comes over to check out Kaylee so I reluctantly release her though I keep my fingers threaded through hers.

Brad walks with them as they wheel Alexis out. Ethan is standing beside me, looking torn. His eyes look between Alexis and Kaylee a couple of times like he is wondering who needs him more.

They decide to take Kaylee in the ambulance to the hospital so they can monitor her. It's just a precaution to make sure all three of them are okay.

I never let go of her hand, which is still shaking, for anything. I make the nurses work around me because I am not leaving her side for a second. I'm afraid to because I'm afraid she will be gone. I have been scared before where Kaylee is concerned, but today, seeing Elizabeth holding a gun at point-blank range aimed at Kaylee is the scariest thing I have ever seen. Thank God, Ethan took control of the situation and saved her life. I hope Alexis' injuries aren't life threatening.

They hook Kaylee up to the monitor to track the babies' heart rates. I'm relieved to hear the sound of their hearts beating.

I bring her hand up and kiss the back of it, thanking God once more that she is okay.

I look at Kaylee, who is staring at the ceiling. "Have you heard if Alexis is okay?" she asks, her eyes never moving from the white painted ceiling.

My thumb strokes the back of her hand. "Sorry, sweetheart, I haven't heard anything."

Kaylee turns her head in my direction, her eyes glistening with tears. "I can't lose her, Adam. She's my best friend."

"She will pull through, Kaylee. She is tough, like someone else I know."

"I was so scared, Adam. I thought my life was over and all I could think about was you and I prayed our babies would make it out okay. I don't want to ever feel like that again."

"It's over now, sweetheart. She is going away for a long time so she can't hurt you anymore," I reassure her. I pray all of this mess is over with. I've had it with people hurting my girl. First, it was Riley, and then the woman who is supposed to be her mother. I can't handle seeing her hurting anymore. She's been through too much in life.

There is a light knock on the door before it leisurely opens. Mom walks in and heads to the other side of the bed to hug Kaylee. Dad walks in behind her and stands next to me. He places his hand on my shoulder and squeezes. Mom continues to talk to Kaylee in hushed tones.

There is another knock on the door then Ethan walks in, closing the door quietly behind him. "Any word on Alexis?" Kaylee asks worriedly.

"She's in surgery now; that is all we know," he replies regretfully. "Adam, I need to talk to you real quick."

I didn't want to let go of Kaylee's hand but judging by the look in his eye, it's important.

"I'll be right back, okay. I will be quick." I lean in, kissing her long and hard, before following Ethan out of the room. "This better be important," I chasten him.

"It is, trust me."

I stop walking when we enter the waiting room. Riley is sitting in a chair in the corner, away from everyone, with his head hunched over. What is he doing here? He had better not think he can be around Kaylee again or that he is in my good graces. I highly doubt we will ever be on good terms.

Ethan leaves the waiting room so he can visit with Kaylee while I figure out what Riley wants.

I kick his foot and his head pops up. His eyes are red and blotchy like he has been crying. I can't tell if it's all an act or if the tears are real.

"How are Alexis and Kaylee doing? And..." He swallows hard. "...the twins, are they okay?" *At least he didn't say 'my kids.'*

Is he serious right now? "I think you lost the right to know anything about them a long time ago," I grind out.

"I know, but it doesn't mean I don't care."

My lips form a thin line. "Right, here's the deal. Unless there is a very good reason why I'm standing here, then get on with it. Otherwise, leave and let me get back to my girl."

"There is, I promise. First, I want to apologize to you for anything I have said or done-"

I cut him off before he could finish. "I'm not the one you should be apologizing to."

He produces a white envelope from his jacket pocket and hands it to me. "I can't and won't go near her so I wrote her a letter, apologizing. I also explained everything to her, why I changed, the agreement I made with her mom, and so on. If she wants to read it, fine. If not, then at least I tried. I'm not looking for forgiveness or to make things right, so don't think that."

I stare at the stark white envelope, studying it, trying to decide if giving it to her is a good idea.

"I also wanted to thank you for being there for her when I wouldn't. I wish I could go back, erase the past eight months, and not take the damn pill. The one tiny object screwed my life up. I promised myself I wouldn't take them; that I wouldn't ruin my life like others have.

Well, I did and I hurt the best thing that ever happened to me.

"Promise me when the kids ask about me that you will tell them the truth. They deserve to know what kind of person I am."

I give him a hard nod. I truly believe he is sorry, but I just can't get over what he did to her.

"I'm going to plead guilty in court on Thursday, just so you know. Elizabeth is going down with me. That's why I kept pushing the trial back. I needed evidence to bring her down."

"I can't guarantee she will read this, but I will give it to her when the time is right."

"That's all I ask." He stands and shoves his hands in his pockets. "Well, I'm going to go so you can get back to her." I watch him as he walks away with his head bowed.

"Riley," I call out before he walks around the corner. He stops and looks over his shoulder, waiting for me to say what I'm going to say. "Thank you for warning us about Elizabeth."

He nods tightly and disappears around the corner.

## Ethan

*"I feel as if my heart has been shot to smithereens."- Ethan*

After spending some time with my sister and making sure her and the twins are okay, I leave to go check on Alexis. Last I heard, she was in surgery. It's been over an hour so maybe she is out now. My heart twists in pain when I remember her lying on the floor unconscious, blood pouring from her stomach. It took me a second to snap out of it, but in the end, I'm thrilled I had knocked the gun out of Elizabeth's hands before she fired another shot.

I found Brad sitting in the same spot he was earlier, his body hunched over and his head bowed. His parents are sitting on each side of him, comforting him. Next to him are Lex's parents. Her mother is softly crying against her husband's shoulder. I feel just as awful as they do, except I keep mine masked. She's not my girl; she's Brad's.

Brad looks up from the floor, his eyes red and blotchy. "I haven't heard anything yet," he murmurs sadly, answering my unspoken question.

"Do you mind if I sit and wait with you?"

He shakes head so I sit a couple of seats down.

"How's Kaylee?"

"She's fine. Shaken, but fine. She keeps asking me about Alexis, but I have nothing to tell her." Yet, another reason why I'm sitting here waiting for the doctor.

"That's good."

I nod in agreement, unsure of what to say now.

Brad clears his throat, gaining my attention. "Thank you."

I just nod again, wondering why he is thanking me. Brad is an all-around good guy. He is good to Lex, and he helps protect my sister. Sometimes, I wish I could find something wrong with him so I could tell Lex that he wasn't good for her, but then I regret thinking it because I want her to be happy. And if Brad is who makes her happy, then I guess I'll be okay.

We wait and we wait for what seems like hours until finally the doctor strolls in and calls Lex's name. I'm the last to jump up from my seat. Her parents and Brad stand before him with hopeful expressions.

The doctor explains she is okay. The bullet missed everything it needed to. He goes on to explain she has lost a lot of blood, but otherwise she is fine, and he expects her to make a full recovery. My shoulders, along with everyone else's, relax, releasing the tension we held in. They all leave to go see her, leaving me to myself. I turn in the opposite direction, making my way back to Kaylee's room to tell her the good news.

I want to follow them but seeing Brad holding her hand, telling her how much he cares for her, would make the pain in my heart grow fiercely. I couldn't handle it.

I visit with Kaylee for a little while, updating her on Alexis. I hug and kiss her cheek before I leave, telling her to let me know when she makes it home.

I leave the hospital feeling like I just left my heart inside. The drive home is a blur and so is whatever else I did before my head hit the pillow.

Alexis haunts my dreams tonight, except this time, she doesn't make it.

I wake up, soaked in a pool of sweat and startled by the disturbing dream I had. My phone rings, and I blindly search for it on the nightstand.

"Yeah," I call out to whoever is on the other line.

"Hey, big brother!" I wince and pull the phone away from my ear. I thought Kaylee was always grumpy in the mornings?

"What's up, sis? How are you so chirpy this morning?"

"I have some awesome news! Alexis is awake and talking!"

I go from being half-asleep, still lying on the bed, to sitting up and wide awake in half a second flat. "That's awesome, Kaylee," I say sounding cool compared to how I really feel.

"I know! We talked for the longest this morning. Anyways, I was wondering if you could do me a favor?"

"What's that?"

"I got her some flowers last night, and I wanted to give them to her when she woke up, but Adam won't let me out of bed so I can't take them to her. Will you take them for me?"

"Yeah, I will." I want to see her so bad. I want to see with my own eyes that she's okay.

"Thanks, Ethan! You're the best!"

I hang up with Kaylee and jump in the shower. I grab a protein shake out of the fridge on my way to the front door.

After picking up the flowers from Kaylee and reassuring her that I will tell Alexis they are from her, I drive to the hospital. Like I want to walk into the room holding flowers I bought her. That's just asking to be decked. If some guy brought my girl flowers, I'd swing first and ask questions later.

The elevator ride seems to be taking its precious time carrying me to the third floor. Finally, I step off the elevator, trying to keep my pace slow. I lightly knock on the door and crack it open. I walk in quietly; I'm surprised she is alone. I didn't think Brad would leave her out of his sight.

I stop walking when she turns her head toward me. She is looking from me to the flowers questionably. Shit, I bet she thinks they are from me.

"Kaylee, uh, asked me to, uh, drop these off for you." I gesture to the flowers she keeps staring at. This has to be one of the most intense moments of my life.

"Thank you," she rasps.

I set the flowers beside the others and step back. I stuff my hands in my pockets leisurely, trying to come up with something to say.

"Where is everyone?" Really, I mean Brad, but it would look suspicious coming from me.

"I told them I needed some time alone. They were suffocating me."

My heart sinks in my chest. "Oh, well, I will get going then." I turn to make my way out the door. My heart is on the verge of exploding in my rib cage.

"I didn't mean you, Ethan," she murmurs softly, stopping me in my tracks.

My heart clenches hearing her say my name.

I turn back around to find her reaching for something on the bedside table. Her face is scrunched together like she is in pain. Whatever she is trying to get is out of reach.

I take the remaining steps to her, pushing her gently back on the bed. "What do you want, Lex?"

Her eyes flash with something I didn't catch. Maybe calling her 'Lex' isn't such a good idea. "My water, please," she whispers, sounding pained.

I pick up her cup and hold it out for her. "Do you need anything else?"

She shakes her head, but something feels off. One of her hands rest on her stomach, her face still scrunched together.

"Lex, are you in pain?"

"A little," she says, her eyes dropping to the blankets covering her.

"Just a little? Why didn't you say something?" I walk around to the other side of her, which has the remote call button. I tell the nurse what she needs and thank her.

The nurse arrives in no time and hands Alexis her pain pill.

"When is everyone coming back?" I ask, mainly out of curiosity. I don't want Brad to think I'm trying to steal his girl. I wish she could be mine, but not when I'm about to deploy in a few months and because I don't do the whole girl cheating on her boyfriend thing. Lex would have to be single for me to pursue her. I'm not going to tell her that though because it would only make her step up her game and shred what little willpower I have left.

"I told them not to come back until I called them. I know it sounds awful but Ethan, between my parents and Brad, I was about to go insane!" she says, throwing her hands up in exasperation.

"They care about you, Alexis. They were scared they were going to lose you," I tell her, stating how I felt yesterday.

"I know they care and they mean well, but they act like I can't do anything. If I coughed, they thought blood was going to come up with it. If I groaned about anything, they thought I was groaning in pain, and they would rush the nurse in like I was dying."

I tried not to laugh at her frustration, but I couldn't help it.

"It's not funny, Ethan! I'm being serious! Not to mention when I tried to take a nap they thought I was dying in front of them!"

I laughed harder at that, causing her to narrow her eyes at me. "I'm sorry for laughing, Lex. It's just it's so damn funny. I can see why you sent them away."

She points to the chair in the corner and says, "You can stay and talk to me for a while if you'd like. At least you don't freak out over me."

I glance briefly back and forth between her and the chair debating whether I should. I give in, walk over, and drag the chair so I can sit next to her. "Do you know when they will discharge you?"

"They said hopefully in a day or two. They just want to make sure my stitches are healing properly and all." She rolls her eyes, picking up her phone out of her lap. She huffs and throws her phone back in her lap.

"Everything okay?"

She pinches the bridge of her nose in irritation. "Even when I tell them to leave me alone, they still text me every thirty minutes to ask me the same question over and over. And then, when I tell them I'm fine, they ask me if I'm sure like five times."

"Lex, you almost died yesterday."

Her eyes grow soft as she fidgets with the blanket covering her. "I know, but I'm fine now. I just want things to go back to normal. How long will they continue to treat me as if I'm made of glass? I mean, you care about me, and you're not acting crazy."

I swallow past the lump in my throat. I do care about her a lot. "I do care, Lex, more than I should." And that's the truth. I care about her more than she will ever know.

We grow silent after that. I find myself wondering what she is thinking about. Did I hurt her feelings? Did I only stir up more of her feelings toward me?

I clear my throat, hoping I can find my voice. "I should, uh, get going. I have some things I need to do."

I stand and move the chair back to where I got it. I move to stand by Lex again, unsure of how I want to say good-bye.

"You don't have to go, you know."

I lean over, pressing my lips to her forehead. Her breath hitches and she closes her eyes. I'm damn near torturing myself right now. "I don't want to leave, but I think it's best for both of us if I do. Do you need anything else before I go?"

She shakes her head and looks away.

I have an overwhelming urge to kiss her so I back away before I follow through.

I grab her phone from her hands, checking to see if she has my number. She doesn't so I program it in there for her. "If you need anything, you have my number," I say as I hand her back her phone.

I pause at the door, looking back at her over my shoulder one last time. She half waves at me, looking sad. It pains me to know that I caused the hurt look on her face.

I close the door behind me and lean against the wall, fighting with myself to walk away and leave her alone. *She has Brad*, my subconscious says. So I walk away from the only girl I could possibly ever want.

*Kaylee*

*"It's game on now, Ethan Harper."- Alexis*

"Prom sucks, Adam." Adam has brought up prom, asking me if I want to go. I really don't see the point since I'm pregnant. Otherwise, I'd be thrilled about going. We are lying in bed wrapped in each other's arms, which is my favorite place to be. My head is in the crook of his neck while his hand is caressing my belly.

"You say that because you haven't been to my prom." He had come up with an idea, but he won't tell me unless I agree to go with him. He knows by now I'm not really a big fan of surprises.

"Tell me about your prom," I encourage him to convince me to go. I would love to go to prom if I wasn't so insecure about my belly standing out for everyone to see.

"Well, it's going to be a sparse crowd. Really sparse. There will definitely be food." Fewer people are good.

"Better be." He chuckles at my demand. "What? I'm pregnant. It's my favorite hobby right now!" I argue.

"I thought I was your favorite hobby?" I shake my head a couple of times. "Damn, I just got booted for food. I'm certainly going to have to up my game." I pull back and look at him. He has the cutest pouty face ever.

I bury my face in his chest and giggle. "In case you've forgotten, I have not one, but two little growing juniors in my belly who require me to eat at least every two to three hours. Besides, when they are born, they will definitely be replacing food as my favorite. Maybe, if you ask nicely, they might share the number one spot."

He scoots down the bed until he is eye level with my stomach. "Hey, you two. Will you please…please…let me split that number one spot with you? I love you both and your momma so much." He leans in and plants two kisses along my rounded belly. I tried to stifle my laughter. "It's never too early to share, either." He leans in, this time to press his ear against my stomach. "What's that? You will? Thanks, you two. That's really nice of you. I love you guys." He kisses them two more times before scooting back up to kiss me. "They said they would love to share," he says with a huge grin. I laugh uncontrollably.

"Well, now that we have got that settled, you still have to convince me to go to prom with you."

"Let's see…I've covered who was going to be there and that we'd have food…" He taps his chin with his finger. "There will be some dancing."

"That sounds boring."

"And some kissing."

Now, I'm intrigued. "Really? What kind of kissing?" I ask teasingly.

"Let me demonstrate." He leans in and captures my mouth with his soft lips. He kisses me slowly and thoughtfully. My hands lock around his neck holding him in place. Adam brings his hands up to cup my face. Each kiss is sweeter than the first. When he stops, he rests his forehead against mine.

"Hmm…I like that kind of kissing."

"Don't worry; I'm positive there will be lots of that," he says matter-of-factly.

"Oh? How can I refuse then?"

"Does that mean you will go to prom with me?" There is so much hope in his voice. I know Adam will make it memorable for me.

"Yes, as long as you keep your promise about the food and the kissing."

He pretends to think for a moment, tapping his index finger against his chin. "I think I can oblige, though I do feel kind of used."

"I can think of other ways to use you," I smirk. My fingers lightly run across his chest seductively.

The sexiest growl I've ever heard rumbles through his chest and up his throat. "Hell, you can use me anytime you want." His mouth eagerly crushes mine. He nips at my bottom lip hungrily.

"Oh, I will," I croak, pulling back. "But it's going to have to wait until tonight. We have a very exciting doctor appointment to get to."

His face plants in the pillow. I laugh and crawl out of bed so I can get dressed.

We have been waiting for this appointment, and now that it's here, I'm so excited I'm shaking. Today, Adam and I get to find out the gender of the twins. Adam and I have both said we don't care if we get either girls or boys just as long as they are healthy. However, he did add that he wouldn't mind having two girls. I told him that he was out of his mind.

I grip Adam's hand in anticipation as the nurse moves the wand around on my belly. We have decided to wait and find out with everyone else this afternoon. Anna is having some cakes made for us to help reveal if they are boys or girls or one of each. On our way home, we have to swing by and drop off the envelope to her so she can make the inside of each cake either pink or blue. Ethan is supposed to pick up the cakes on his way to our house this afternoon.

It's been a week since my mother tried to kill me. Alexis has been out of the hospital for a few days. From what she's saying, she's about ready to pull her hair out. I know how she feels because Adam barely lets me do anything as well. The only time he allows me out of bed is for school, to use the bathroom, and to shower. I tried to tell him that I'm more than fine, but he is still clinging to what the nurse said before she discharged me from the hospital. "Now be careful about overdoing it. If you show any signs of preterm labor or have any pain or bleeding, then come back immediately." I guess Adam thinks if I move a muscle, I will start to have problems. I know he loves me and he wants all of us to be healthy so I try to let it go and let him take care of us.

The dreaded trial is in a few days so I'm trying to focus on today so I won't be constantly thinking about if Riley is actually going to show up, and if he does show, what the outcome will be.

Once we are finished with the doctor and we have dropped off the envelope to the cake decorator, Adam drives to Elizabeth's house. This time there will be nothing standing in my way of getting my things. Her trial date is set for next month when the judge decides how long she will be put away for. Good riddance.

"Are you sure you want to go in here?" Adam asks me. We are standing outside the front door of the house that holds many painful memories for me.

"I'll be fine. You?"

"As long as you are, I will be, sweetheart." He places a feather-like kiss to my temple before opening the door and leading me through.

The room is still as I remember it. Even Alexis' blood is still on the carpet.

I start with my closet, gathering all of the clothes and shoes I want to take with me. Adam is next to me, making sure I don't reach for anything above my head.

I notice a book I don't ever remember seeing on the top shelf so I ask Adam to reach it for me.

"*Disney's Classic Stories*," I read aloud. "Dad used to read me a story every night from this book for the longest time." I don't remember putting it up there after we moved. I open the book and something falls out of it. Adam picks it up off the floor for me and hands it to me. I hand Adam the book so I can open the mysterious parchment.

It looks like some kind of agreement; I'm just not sure what it says. Dad and Elizabeth's signatures are at the bottom of it though so it has to be important.

"What's it say, Kaylee?"

"I'm not sure. See if you can figure it out."

He takes it from me and scans the document. "I think this is a deed of some sort. It looks like to a house. You might want to call Ethan to see if he knows anything."

"I don't know what house it could be to, Adam. Elizabeth sold the other house to pay for this one."

"I don't know, sweetheart. Call Ethan while I finish gathering your stuff."

I pull out my phone from my back pocket and dial his number. I try to explain to him what I found, but I just keep confusing him so he says he will swing by. While we wait on Ethan to arrive, I start going through my desk to make sure there is nothing important. I grab the pictures I have of Dad and me. My eyes mist as I look through them. I miss him so much. I hate that he is not here to watch me grow up.

In my peripheral, I see Adam walking over to me. He stands behind me, his hands massaging my arms as he peers over my shoulder. "Remember what I said, sweetheart. He is always with you."

"I know. I just wish he was here," I murmur sadly.

"Knock, knock, sis," Ethan says as he enters my old room. "What's this weird paper you're trying to ask me about? Quite badly, I might add."

Adam hands him the unknown document, and Ethan scans it over.

"What?" I ask when I see him grin widely.

"Well, sis, according to this, you are a homeowner."

"You're lying," I chasten him.

"I'm serious, Kaylee. This is the deed to the old house," Ethan says proudly.

"That makes no sense. Elizabeth sold it to pay for this one," I explain, telling him the same thing I told Adam.

"You sure about that? If this is real, which I'm a hundred positive it is, there is no way she can sell it because it's not in her name."

I need to sit down. I sit down in my desk chair, trying to comprehend the news he just delivered. "What do I need to do now?"

Adam speaks up. "Well, this weekend you and I can drive down and check out the house."

"Plus, Dad's lawyer friend can probably give you some insight as well," Ethan adds.

"Okay, sounds good. I need to visit Dad again anyway."

We finish packing my stuff so we can head home. I know I can speak for Adam when I say I'm anxious to see what color the cakes will be.

## 23

*Kaylee*

*"Want to know something crazy? I almost told Kaylee I loved her once." –Riley*

"How about Jasmine for our little girl?" I ask Adam out of the blue.

We are lying in our bed, facing each other. Adam's hand is caressing my belly. Neither of us has said much as we are just staring at one another, enjoying each other's company. Anna is running some errands and Jack is at the shop. Adam chose to stay home with me this morning since I was running to the bathroom every thirty minutes or so, throwing my guts up. I threw up my breakfast and the crackers I had eaten that were supposed to calm my stomach.

"Jasmine," he tests out the name. "I like it. It's a beautiful name for our beautiful baby girl."

We found out we are having a girl and a boy so we are thinking of names for our little miracles. The cakes looked amazing yesterday, and they tasted wonderful, too. The lady who made them did an amazing job. She made two round eight-inch cakes. She covered them with white icing and had pink and blue question marks all over them. Adam and I both cut each cake, revealing the blue first.

"Jasmine Alexis Thomas," I try out her full name and grin at Adam. The day Adam and I had first started discussing names, I asked him if it would be okay if our little girl had Alexis' middle name. He agreed without a second thought. Alexis doesn't know yet and I do not plan to tell her until we are sure of the names we pick out. "Now we just need to come up with a name for our little man."

Both of us are quiet as we try to come up with a boy's name. I kind of want to stick with the letter J since they are twins.

Adam is the first one to come up with a name. "How about Jackson Blake Thomas?"

I ponder on it for a moment. My lips curl into a smile. "It's perfect. He will be as..." I trail off, noticing what I was about to say. I can't believe I almost said that.

Adam leans forward and kisses my forehead. "Hey, sweetheart. What's wrong?"

"Nothing," I reply, knowing that he knows I'm lying.

"Talk to me, Kaylee," he says softly.

"I just about said something really stupid," I whisper.

"What was it?"

I drop my gaze, not wanting to see his reaction. "I just about said that he will be as handsome as his dad."

"Hey." He nudges my chin up with fingers. "They may not have my genes or my looks, but they are still mine. Nothing will change that, sweetheart."

"I know, but I was afraid if I had said it you would've thought I was talking about..." I don't say his name because it reminds me of a horrible time in my life.

Adam shakes his head. "You know why? Because I know when you think of their dad, you think of me. If you had said it, I probably would've said something like, 'Of course, he will be as handsome as me.'" He laughs and I giggle.

"You're amazing, you know that?" He really is. I couldn't ask for anyone better to be by my side.

He rolls his eyes, like he knows this already. "Well, yeah," he says sarcastically.

I shake my head. "You and your ego."

"You love me and my ego."

"Only because I love everything about you."

Adam leans down and captures my mouth with a heart-stopping kiss. My hand comes up and rests on his cheek. "And I love you more, sweetheart."

Adam and I are on our way to visit with Dad. We just left from speaking to a lawyer about the house and Dad's car, which I thought Elizabeth had sold. She said we were broke, and my little car was all we could afford. Yeah, right. She was keeping the house and the car for her…after she killed me, or so it seemed. I'm not exactly sure what she planned to do with it. That is hard to come to terms with. Elizabeth had been hiding money for years. There were months she would whine about how the electricity might be turned off or how we might have to stretch our food supply out for another week or two. I can't believe her! Surely, Dad didn't know her true colors. I don't believe he would have stayed with her if he knew. I can't believe I even bought her lies. I was so out of it for a long time in the beginning since I was struggling with losing Dad. Now that I'm healing, I see who she has been all along.

Adam and I stroll hand in hand to Dad's grave. It hurts my heart every time I visit and there are times when the blame tries to creep its way in. Now, I just push it aside and continue my day like normal.

"Hey, Dad," I say, just like all the other times I visit. "You probably know this already, but I'm going to tell you anyway to get it off my chest." I pause to take a deep breath. "Ever since you were taken from me, I've blamed myself. Not a day went by that I didn't think if I had just said 'Okay' and waited until the next day when you felt better that you'd still be here. I know now that it wasn't my fault. It's taken me four years to realize it, but I finally have. We were simply in the wrong place at the wrong time." I run my hand over my swollen belly. "I wish you were here to see your grandchildren. I promise I will talk about you all the time and tell them about all the times you and I had a tea party and about how extravagant my birthday parties were." I smile as I think back, remembering.

"I know you will watch over Jackson and Jasmine and protect them like you have for me. I love you, Daddy. I miss you more than you can imagine. I wish you were here with us, but I know that if you were still here, I wouldn't have Adam. Adam saved me, Dad; he pulled me from the darkness I was lost in. He supports me, encourages me, but most of all, he loves me, and he loves Jackson and Jasmine. Despite the things that have happened, he's still here. I wish you could meet him," I whisper sadly, glancing back at Adam, who is leaning against a tree watching me intently. His lips curl into the smile that I love.

I look back at the inscription on the marble stone. "I love you, Dad. I'll see you soon."

I wave Adam over to help me stand. Knowing my luck, I'll try to stand and fall right back down. He pulls me to my feet and kisses my hair. Adam walks me a few feet away then stops. "Give me a couple of minutes, I'll be right back." He walks back over to Dad and talks to him. His lips are moving though I can't make out what he is saying. Occasionally, he'll glance over at me and smile like he is talking about me to Dad. When he is done, he pats Dad's tombstone and makes his way back to me.

We walk hand in hand back to Adam's truck. I want to ask him what he said to Dad, but it's really none of my business. Dad and Adam would've gotten along great. I smile to myself, imagining what it would be like to see them interact with each other.

"What are you smiling about, sweetheart?" Adam asks as he stops at a red light.

"I was just thinking about what it'd be like for you and Dad to hang out."

Adam grasps my hand and brings it to his mouth. "I believe we'd get along just fine. Of course, that would be after he put the fear of God in me," Adam says with a laugh.

I giggle. "Yeah, I can totally see that happening. Dad may not look mean, but he would be if he had to, though I've never seen it firsthand."

"Probably because you were his baby girl and he had a hard time getting mad at you. From what you have told me about him, he had a hard time telling you no," Adam jokes. I know he didn't mean for it to be an insult, but his comment hit me the wrong way. "Hey," Adam says softly. "I'm sorry, I shouldn't have said that."

"It's okay, I know you didn't mean for it to hurt. You're right, Dad did have a hard time telling me no. I wish that day, he would have for once."

Adam pulls into an empty parking spot at the diner I used to eat at when I had friends. "Me too, sweetheart," he murmurs, leaning across the console to kiss me. Adam hops out of the truck and walks around to open the door for me. Once he helps me out, his hand slides down my arm to grab my hand. Adam holds the door open for me, letting me walk in first while never letting go of my hand.

We pick a booth by the window and sit down. It is hard for me to scoot over with my huge belly weighing me down, but I manage to do it.

"Are you feeling all right, sweetheart?" Adam asks his usual question.

"Just a little tired. Other than that, I'm fine," I assure him.

The waitress comes over and takes our drink order. Adam's phone rings just as the waitress walks away. He mouths 'mom' to me, letting me know who it is. While he is talking to Anna, I glance around the diner at the other patrons. I see a couple with a toddler sitting a few tables down from us, happily smiling. At another table, another couple is gazing at each, lost in each other's eyes. The people at the next table have me blinking a few times to make sure I'm not seeing things. It's been years since I've seen or talked to them. They don't seem to have changed much over the years. I turn my focus back to Adam, who is hanging up with his mother, hoping I will go unnoticed by them. The way I see it, we have nothing left to say to each other. They left me on my own to deal with losing the most important person in my life.

"Kaylee," Adam's voice snaps me out of my lingering thoughts. "What would you like to eat, sweetheart?" The way Adam is watching me; I know he knows something is bothering me.

I give the waitress my order and she leaves. I wait patiently for Adam to start trying to figure out what's wrong.

"What are you thinking about, sweetheart?" His hand moves across the table and clasps mine. My gaze drifts back over to the girls that I used to know. Adam follows my gaze and then looks back at me with a questioning expression. "Who are they, Kaylee?"

My eyes drift back to his. "Just some people I used to know," I murmur, shrugging like it's no big deal. Adam knows differently, though. Thankfully, the waitress brings our appetizers at that moment, relieving me of having to answer any questions.

I eat my food quickly, hoping Adam does the same so we can get out of here.

Every so often, I glance over at their table to see if they are still there. To my dismay, they are.

After the waitress brings us our ticket, Adam leaves to go pay it. Out of the corner of my eye, I see them stand from their table and gather their stuff to leave. I let my hair fall in front of my face, hoping they won't recognize me.

"Kaylee, is that you?" the voice I recognize as Hannah's asks in surprise.

I lift my head and turn toward them, giving them a slight smile. "Hey, Hannah, Holly."

Both seem unsure of what to say. "How have you been? We haven't seen you in a while," Hannah finally says. In the beginning, they would ask me how I was doing but, as soon as I'd answer negatively, we'd fall into an uncomfortable silence.

I almost want to snort at the words 'a while.' It's been longer than that. All three of us were once inseparable, but like my brother and my mother, they turned on me. Our everyday calls quit, and once they stopped calling, they eventually stopped talking to me altogether.

"I'm doing pretty well." I look past them wondering where Adam is. Shouldn't he be back already?

"Do you mind if we sit?" Holly asks pointing to the empty seats across from me.

"Sure," I mumble.

Adam arrives and slides in next to me. Hannah and Holly's eyes widen when they see him. "Hannah, Holly, this is Adam, my boyfriend." Adam, being Adam, shakes their hand. It isn't lost on me that they are still ogling him.

Hannah clears her throat as her eyes drop to my stomach, something I notice both of them have done several times already. "Congratulations, by the way. When are you due?"

I just stare at her because it's funny that they think we can just pick up our friendship. "I'm not trying to be rude, but both of you turned your backs on me when I needed you. You were my best friends and you just dropped our friendship like it meant nothing to you." I sigh and scrub my face with my hands. "I guess what I'm trying to say is that I don't understand how you can just act like nothing has changed, like it hasn't been four years since you've said a word to me."

Adam moves his arm around my shoulders, letting his fingers trail up and down my arm. He is trying to soothe me, make sure I stay calm, and I love him for that. I don't need to get all worked up and stressed out.

The girls look at me with remorse. "Maybe we should have tried harder, but when we were told you didn't want to talk to anyone, we decided not to push. We knew you were going through a tough time so we thought it'd be best if we waited for you to decide if you wanted to talk. Then you left without telling us and we had no idea where you moved to." Holly's words tumble around in my mind. I know I never told them I didn't want to see them, just like I never told Ethan.

I think I just figured out the problem, but I needed to hear it from them. "Who told you that I didn't want any visitors?"

"Your mom was the one who told us." I don't respond; I just lay my head on Adam's shoulder. Ethan, my friends, Alexis...what happened to Elizabeth? What made her turn evil?

Adam curses under his breath and I clench my fists together under the table.

"We're really sorry, Kaylee. We thought we were doing what you wanted," Holly murmurs and I feel bad for them. I always thought the reason nobody came to see me was because I was to blame. That was never the truth; my mother had turned them all away with the same story.

"It's not your fault," I assure them. "I've recently found out some things that were shocking, to say the least." I hope they don't want me to elaborate. Otherwise, we will be sitting here all evening.

"Where are you living now?"

"Bowling Green." I don't offer any more; I just leave it at that.

Holly and Hannah look at each other before Hannah speaks. "Well, we need to get going, but we want to visit you again, Kaylee, and you know, catch up. That's if you want to," she adds quickly.

I smile at both of them. "It would be good to talk to you girls again."

We exchange numbers and I even hug both of them, promising to get in touch with them soon.

On the ride home, I think of how different my life could have been. I would still be lost, but not as bad as I would have been without my friends.

## Adam

*"Lex's face flashes in my mind every time I'm with Kate. God, this girl gets under my skin like nobody can."-Ethan*

The darn note has been burning a hole in my hands. I've been sitting here staring at it, wondering if the right time to give it to her is now. I don't know how she will react to it. Kaylee may get pissed and think I have been keeping things from her again. The trial is tomorrow morning and I know it's been weighing on her mind. It has mine too, even though I know the outcome. He seemed sincere when he said he would plead guilty, but it doesn't mean he won't change his mind. Riley may chicken out about going to jail. Who knows what he is really going to do?

I sit on the edge of my bed, waiting for Kaylee to emerge from the shower. The fear of her leaving me over this stupid letter is gnawing at my insides. It's slowly eating me alive. I've already lost her once, and it's not something I want to feel again, ever.

Kaylee breezes into the bedroom her and I share, towel drying her hair. She is dressed in yoga pants and an old t-shirt, ready for bed. Her perfectly round stomach catches my attention. We are now over halfway through her pregnancy. Jackson and Jasmine, the names we have picked out for them, will be here in around four months. By then, everything should be behind us so we can start our life together. Elizabeth, and hopefully Riley, will be locked away so they can't hurt my girl anymore. We will have graduated high school, even though I know Kaylee still wishes she could drop out and get her GED. Thankfully, everyone at school is finally leaving her alone. I believe it was Riley telling them to pick on her, but I'm not positive. They still whisper behind her back, trying to spread rumors. I told Kaylee I didn't care what they said because I loved her and I knew the truth.

"What's that?" she asks, pointing to the stark white envelope burning my hands. I knew this moment would come; I'm just not ready for it. Ethan, Brad, and I haven't told the girls about Riley coming to us and warning us about Elizabeth. I imagine now it's about to change. I can't tell her where I got the letter without telling her the whole story.

I pat the spot on the bed next to me, inviting her to sit. "Come here, sweetheart."

She eyes me suspiciously but doesn't argue.

"I want you to hear me out, all right? Please, listen to what I have to say before you jump to conclusions." I know I'm scaring her, but I need her to keep an open mind.

"Okay," she murmurs.

"This is a letter…from Riley," I say slowly.

Her eyes dart to the letter I'm clutching in my hands. "I don't understand. How did you get that?"

"I'm going to start from the beginning, okay?" She nods so I begin the story. "The day you and Alexis were at Elizabeth's, Riley came to the house warning us about Elizabeth. At first, we all laughed because we didn't know you and Alexis were there." She starts to interrupt, but I cut her off. "Brad didn't see Alexis' text until he pulled out his phone to call her."

She shakes her head. "I'm sorry, Adam, but I can't see him doing that."

"I couldn't believe it either, Kaylee, but I'm telling the truth. Riley saved you both."

Her eyes mist over as she continues to shake her head back and forth. "Riley isn't that person. He doesn't have the heart to save someone, especially me."

"Ask your brother. Hell, call Brad and ask him. They will both tell you the exact same thing I just told you. I know it's hard to comprehend, sweetheart, but if it weren't for him…" I swallow hard, finding it hard to finish the sentence. "Let's just say I'd be visiting you and your father at the same time."

"When did he give you the letter?" she prompts.

"Remember when we were in the hospital and Ethan stuck his head in saying that he needed me?"

"Yeah."

"Riley was sitting in the waiting room, wanting to talk to me. He handed me this and said for me to give it to you. I told him I would, but I couldn't promise him that you'd read it. I wanted to wait until the right moment to give it to you because I didn't know how you would react, but I realized there wouldn't be a perfect moment."

"What does it say?"

"I don't know. I haven't opened it because it's none of my business. If you want me to read it first, I will. Just tell me what you want to do with it."

"You can read it, that way you can decide if it will be okay for me to or not."

"I'm not going to say whether you can or you can't read it. It's entirely up to you to decide. I can tell you what it's about, but you need to decide if you want to read it."

I grab one of her hands and kiss it before ripping open the envelope. I breathe in deeply, letting it out slowly. Here goes nothing.

*Dear Kaylee,*

*Where do I begin? How do I even begin to tell you how sorry I am for hurting you, for hitting you, for everything. I despised every second of it, but I didn't have a choice. I made the worst decision of my life and you had to pay for it, and for that I can't even begin to describe how awful I feel. I'm not looking for forgiveness. I don't expect you to ever forgive me.*

*When I first saw you, I knew I wanted you. You kept turning me down, but I didn't want to give up on the idea of there being an us. You were never a conquest to me. From the very beginning, you ignited something in me. You were different, you were innocent, and you were like a breath of fresh air. I wanted, needed a change, and you were it.*

*It felt surreal when you finally said yes to me. I didn't care who made fun of me, who laughed at me, or what anyone said about me being with you. After asking you all throughout our junior year, you finally gave me a chance. I never wanted to screw it up, but I did anyways.*

*This is the part where I wish I could go back and change everything. You see, I turned to the one thing I told myself I would stay away from. Drugs. My parents, mainly my father, were constantly riding me about something. For Dad, it was football and my performance on the field. For Mom, it was getting a full ride to a university I didn't even want to attend and getting a degree I had no interest in. This is what happens when you have wealthy, good for nothing parents who only want you to do the things they decide. I was stressed to the max and I thought I could get them off my back if I performed my best, but in order to perform my best to their expectations, I needed help. And this is where I screwed up. I should have said screw it and screw them, but I didn't. Looking back, it wouldn't have mattered how much they yelled at me because I had you to keep me sane. You always knew what to say to take my mind off it. If I had just thought of you, I wouldn't have taken the first pill. I got steroids from some guy I didn't know, thinking I'd only take a few. A few turned into ten, which turned into twenty. I became addicted and soon, I racked up a whopping five grand in debt with no way to pay for it. It turns out those little round things cost a lot and then there is interest. I couldn't go ask my parents for it without them wondering what it was for and my inheritance didn't kick in until I turned eighteen. I was up shit creek. Also, I didn't realize the side effects of those damn pills either.*

*One night, I was walking to my car and I was jumped. Needless to say, I was given two choices. I pay them their money or I die. No sooner than they had left did your mother walk up to me and I thought, 'Oh shit.'*

*Here is where the story takes an abrupt turn. I thought she was going to yell at me for not being good for you, but I was wrong on so many levels. Elizabeth offered me a way out...for a price.*

*The price was you. She would pay my debt if I started being mean to you, as in become controlling and constantly finding something to yell at you for. I thought maybe I could do it for a while then beg you for forgiveness. I soon learned my mistake, but it was too late. I was indebted to her so whatever she ordered me to do, I had to follow through with it. I was stuck with no way out.*

*Her next assignment was for me to break you, mentally and physically. Elizabeth was sick and twisted for sure, but I noticed way too late. Each time I would hit you, I'd have to leave. I couldn't stay there knowing what I just did. I couldn't stay around for fear I'd confess and ruin everything. Then both of us would be killed.*

*When Adam started pursuing you, I hated it. I was dead set on begging you to take me back so I feared that if I sat back and let him win you over, I'd lose you forever. I was a selfish prick. Plus, Elizabeth thought it was another fun way to mess with you. Now, I see he is the one for you. I wish things were different so I could be the one who makes you happy, but that's my fault.*

*When Elizabeth came to me with her next assignment, I literally threw up at her feet. I tried to come up with what I owed her so I could pay her off and get out, but as you know, I didn't succeed in doing that. I still feel sick knowing what I took from you. I know there were times I would push you, but it was all an act. It was part of another me I had to create, if that makes sense.*

*I didn't tell you any of this to feel sorry for me. I don't want you to because I don't deserve you, and I sure as hell don't deserve to walk around like I'm innocent. Which is why I'm going to plead guilty in court. I thought I would feel relief when I paid her off, but it still didn't make what I did any better.*

*Again, I'm sorry. I know no matter how many times I apologize, it won't change a thing. Knocking you up was never part of the plan. I'm glad Adam is by your side and that he can be the man you need when I couldn't. If the kids ever ask about me, make sure you tell them the ugly truth. I don't want you to sugarcoat it for them because they deserve to know what a piece of shit I am.*

*I have no doubt you will be a wonderful mother, Kaylee. You are so patient and so kind. So don't worry, you got this.*

*Riley*

I fold the letter and pass it to Kaylee who has been watching me read it.

"Is it bad?"

"No, he explains things. Not that it discounts what he did, but he's apologizing to you."

"Oh," she murmurs, seeming surprised. She takes the note from me and opens it.

I watch her like she did me, gauging her reaction. Her eyes fill with unshed tears, but she keeps reading. I thumb away the tears that slide down her cheek, wondering if it actually was a bad idea to let her read it.

When she's done, she refolds the letter and closes her eyes, laying her head on my shoulder. "So, it really was Elizabeth behind it all."

"Unfortunately, sweetheart, but you won't have to worry about her anymore."

She lifts her head off my shoulder, her eyes finding mine. "He won't change his mind about tomorrow, will he?"

There is so much hope and fear in that one sentence. "I don't think so. He knows he screwed up, and he knows he has to pay for it."

"Why couldn't he have talked to me about his problems?"

"I don't know, Kaylee. That is something only he could tell you. Maybe he was afraid you would leave him. Who knows, sweetheart."

She grows silent, her head back on my shoulder. I just hold her in my arms, reassuring her that I'm here for her.

She knows I love her and I know without a doubt she loves me, but damn, it hurts to sit here knowing that she is thinking of how things could have been. I don't want to know what life would be like without her in it. She and I met for a reason and I thank the good Lord above for bringing us together.

## 25

*Kaylee*

*"Every time I feel him looking at me, my skin crawls."- Kaylee*

I keep my eyes strained forward, trying to block out Riley, who is seated to my right. He keeps looking at me every so often. I can feel the weight of his gaze on me every time his eyes shift my way. Not to mention Adam releases a low growl each time. I still can't get over the fact that Riley saved us. The idea is hard to wrap my head around. The old Riley would have without a doubt, but the new Riley, who is currently burning a hole through my side, wouldn't. I just can't see it. I thought Adam was playing a sick joke on me at first until I called Ethan…and Brad later, who both told me the exact same thing, like Adam said they would.

I still don't know what to make of his letter. I know I can't forgive him for putting me through what he did. I don't know if I ever will. Maybe in time, who knows? He claims he is turning himself in today, but I'm not holding my breath until I hear him say it. He could back out at any given moment and try to get out of it. He could turn the tables and try to pin it all on me somehow.

And Elizabeth, where do I start with her? I still don't even know if she really blamed me for Dad's death or if it was all an act the whole time. I don't know what I've done to her to make her hate me so much. Is it the money Dad left me? Is it really because Dad was killed? I guess I will find out when I go visit her. Maybe she will actually tell me the truth.

We all rise for the judge as he walks in and takes his seat. My hands fidget in front of me, reminding me how nervous and scared I am. I am not looking forward to getting on the stand and testifying. If Riley pleads guilty, I shouldn't have to. It's still hard to talk about it regardless but having to get up in front of a room full of people is petrifying.

After we sit back down, the judge summons Riley to stand and ask him how he pleads. I draw in a harsh breath, waiting for the bomb to drop. So much has happened in my life that I automatically start assuming the worst now. It's a new habit I want to break. My eyes lock on the judge as I wait to hear his answer. The only noise you hear is someone clearing their throat, someone shifting in their seat, and the harsh whispering from Riley's parents.

"Guilty," Riley says in a low, hoarse voice. All the tension leaves my body, and it sags from the release of pressure. All the shocked gasps from his side of the court fill the room.

Adam leans forward, kissing my hair, and I want to cry in relief.

It's finally over. I didn't think this day would ever come.

The remainder of the session seems to pass quickly after that. The judge sets a date for his sentencing and he is read his rights. I hear them cuff him and, unfortunately for me, when they take him out of the courtroom, they walk right in front of me. He looks straight at me with his dead eyes. At the beginning of our relationship, those eyes used to make me smile, make my heart feel these crazy emotions. Now, when I look at them, all I see are those cold eyes peering down at me from above.

We manage to escape without feeling the wrath of his parents. My left arm links with Alexis' while Adam holds my hand firmly in his grasp on my right. Brad is walking next to Alexis while Ethan and Adam's parents form a line behind us. We do, however, run into Luke in the parking lot. I think he had been waiting for us, judging by the fact he was leaning against my car. Luke is one of Riley's best friends, or was. I'm not sure if they are still friends or not. He lights a cigarette just as we approach him.

"What do you want, Luke?" Adam asks as we slow to a stop a few feet away. Brad and Ethan step around to stand in front of Alexis and me.

He takes a long drag off his cigarette. "I wanted to apologize." Oh hell, what now? "I, uh, lied to the cops."

I tighten my grip on Adam's hand. "How exactly did you lie?" Adam grinds out.

"Riley told them that he was with me and I went along-" Adam rips his hand from mine and has Luke pinned against my car before he could finish.

"Adam!" I scream his name hoping he would let him go. The last thing I need is for him to be locked up for fighting. We are outside the courthouse for goodness' sake.

"I'm sorry, I didn't know he was going to take it as far as he did," he chokes out under the pressure of Adam's arm against his throat.

Brad and Ethan finally pry him off Luke, hauling him back.

"What in the hell are you talking about?"

He knew and he still let it happen?

Luke breathes in deeply, running his hands through his hands before spilling his secrets. "A few days before it happened, he was saying how he was going to make her give it up to him. I laughed it off because I didn't think he was serious." He rubs his face with his hand. "When he called me and told me that he got it, I thought she finally caved. Then he told me to tell the police when they called that he had been with me. When I asked him what he did, he just laughed it off and told me that he would make my life hell if I didn't lie. Man, I'm sorry. This has been eating me alive since I covered for him. When the cop told me what he was accused of, I felt sick. Every time I saw you two, I wanted to say something, but I couldn't."

"You're sorry? All of this is your fault, Luke! She almost died because of you!"

"I understand what I did is unforgivable-"

"You're damn right, it is! You have no idea the amount of pain you have caused, not only to her but to me, my parents, her brother, and Alexis! When I saw her face, my heart broke. At first, she wouldn't tell any of us what he did because he threatened to kill her if she told! Then when I found the other bruises, my heart shattered into a million pieces! When the nurses took her from me, I was so wounded I couldn't even tell them anything! My father had to speak for me! When I found out what else he did, it took every damn ounce of strength I had not to go and kill him! It was more than just the physical hurt he caused her! Many nights she couldn't sleep because when she closed her eyes, she relived every painful moment! So no, I don't forgive you! I hope this haunts you until you die!"

"Lucas Adam Thomas!" his mother scolds.

They carry on like Anna didn't say a word. "I'm so sorry, Adam."

"Sorry is not going to take it back, Luke. Besides, I'm not the one you should be apologizing to."

I step forward, threading my fingers through Adam's, hoping to calm him down. When I notice it doesn't help, I cup his face in my hands and force him to look at me. "Adam, can you please calm down. None of this matters anymore. It's over, remember?"

He leans forward, resting his forehead against mine. His arms snake around my waist, molding me to him. Adam takes a few calming breaths before speaking. "It's over," he whispers, reminding himself that Riley is now in jail.

"Yes."

Like this, we are in our own little bubble, our own little world. The world around us fades, leaving just the two of us wrapped in each other's arms.

Adam tilts his head up to kiss my forehead. "I'm sorry for losing it, sweetheart."

"I love you," I murmur.

He smiles. "Love you more."

"Impossible."

"Believe it, sweetheart."

I roll my eyes. "Whatever."

Luke walks away without another word with his head bowed. I actually kind of feel sorry for Luke. As long as I have known him, he has always been kind to me.

"I'll be right back," I tell Adam and walk away. I walk as fast as my pregnant self will let me to catch up with Luke. "Luke!" I yell, gaining his attention.

He stops and slowly turns around to face me, keeping his eyes cast downward.

"I just wanted you to know that I forgive you, Luke."

Luke shakes his head. "You don't have to say it because you feel sorry for me."

"You got it all wrong. The reason I forgive you is because I know you're not a bad person. You just happened to be caught up in the wrong crowd. To be honest, if you had told the truth, nothing would've changed, you see because Riley had already accomplished what he set out to do."

"It still doesn't make what I did okay."

"No, it doesn't, but I still forgive you."

"Thanks, Kaylee."

"Anytime."

I walk back to Adam and the rest of the gang to find his mother scolding him.

"I don't want to ever see you do something like that again. Do you understand me?" she chastens.

"Yes, ma'am," he replies sullenly, reaching for my hand.

We all end up at Adam's, well, our house, for lunch. The guys all start chatting about cars while we girls are discussing prom. Alexis and I make plans to go dress shopping tomorrow after school since prom is next Saturday night.

I can't wait to see what Adam has planned for just the two of us. I'm actually looking forward to this one surprise.

## 26

### Kaylee

*"All the flutters, the kicks, make me fall in love with Jasmine and Jackson that much more. It feels so surreal."-Kaylee*

I'm so full of nerves right now waiting on five o'clock. That's what time Adam and I are supposed to leave for the prom. After sitting in a chair for two hours while Alexis worked her magic on my hair and make-up, I was ready to go. I waited until a few days before to buy the dress since I'm retaining extra pounds every week. I'm only twenty-three weeks pregnant, but yet I still feel huge. Anna laughs at me and says I haven't seen huge yet. Like that makes me feel any better.

"Baby girl, you are smoking! Wait until Adam sees you! He will go nuts!" my best friend squeals with excitement. I just roll my eyes and shake my head.

I chose a strapless pale pink dress that stopped just passed my knees with pink flats. There was no way I was going to wear heels tonight.

The doorbell rings, making my stomach swell with nerves. Alexis walks out first then she links her arm in mine, practically dragging me with her. *It's just Adam. Get a grip!* I mentally tell myself. Everyone is waiting in the living room. Adam, Brad, and Ethan are the first to stand. All three guys stare with their mouths hanging open. Alexis and I just laugh at their reaction.

"God, you're breathtaking," Adam croons when he finally walks over to me. "Are you feeling okay?" Oh, Adam, such a worrier.

I beam at him. "I feel great."

"Oh, here." He takes the corsage out of its package and slides it on my left wrist.

"Thank you, it's perfect." I tilt my head up and kiss him on the mouth.

Ethan makes his way around Adam and pulls me into a hug. "You look beautiful, sis." When he pulls back, he cuts his eyes to Alexis, who is watching us. "Both of you do." He kisses her on her cheek as well. I look at Brad, who flexes his jaw tightly. Oh, no. This can't be good. Alexis must've noticed it too because she says good-bye to Adam's parents and leaves with Brad in tow.

Once we finished eating, Adam and I make our way back to his truck. "Where are we going?" I ask once we had started down the road.

"It's a surprise." His eyes twinkle with glee. Mine narrow in slits at him in response. He knows I hate surprises. I've made it known on more than one occasion.

Adam parks his truck by the meter and gets out. Looking around, I assess the place. Befuddled, I glance nervously at Adam, who is now in front of me with the biggest grin on his face. "Where are we?"

He responds by saying, "Close your eyes, sweetheart."

I obey, letting him lead me down the sidewalk. We walk for what feels like a mile before I hear a door creak open and shut behind us. "Open your eyes, sweetheart." His breath tickles my ear.

When I open my eyes, I gasp. My heart leaps in my chest. I couldn't believe it; I couldn't believe Adam did this all for me. Tears burn in my eyes as I look around the studio. Twinkling lights, balloons, flowers, and streamers transform the studio I used to dance in as a kid. The lighting is dim, setting the mood for a romantic evening. Not wanting to ruin my make-up, I blink back the tears.

Realizing I haven't said a word, I turn back around to face Adam. He stands, silently gauging my reaction. His hands are stuffed in his pockets as he watches me. I open my mouth to speak, but the words lodge in my throat. He nods in understand while striding toward me, taking me in his arms. All the memories from long ago, when my father would drop me off and pick me up, come flooding back. "I love you so much. Thank you." His head descends to mine, capturing it vehemently.

Then a thought hits me. "How did you pull this off without me knowing?"

He shrugged absentmindedly. "I had some help."

As the night goes on, we dance, we kiss, and we laugh. Adam and I are having the time of our lives at our own little prom that he'd created. We only play songs that speak to each other.

I'm not ready to go home, but I feel drained, like I'd overdone it tonight. Adam helps me out of my dress and massages my feet for me since they ache a little. We murmur 'I love you' and I fall asleep snuggled against Adam with a smile plastered on my face.

I wake the next morning with the weight of Adam's arm slinked around me. I turn on my other side so our faces are inches apart. He looks so peaceful, so calm in his sleep. My finger lightly traces over his features. When I reach his lips, he stirs, grabbing my hand and kissing it lightly. "Good morning, beautiful." Adam starts his normal morning routine. First, he would tell me good morning and kiss me, and then he would rub my belly and tell the babies good morning. Finally, he would kiss my belly before giving me one more kiss. He does this every morning.

Ethan shows up later that morning looking exasperated. I thought about asking what was wrong, but I feel as if I already know. "Has she called you?" He lets out a frustrated sigh when I shake my head. Ethan sits down on the couch, joining Adam while he watches TV. I try to call Alexis, but it goes straight to voicemail. I'm sure she's all right, but that doesn't stop the troubling thoughts that run through my mind.

A little after noon, I finally get a call from Alexis. I walk out of the living room so Ethan doesn't hear me talking to her. "Hey, where are you...oh, you're at Brad's...okay, see you in a bit." I hang up to find an awaiting Ethan in front of me.

"Well?" he asks.

"She will be here in a little while."

"She stayed with him." It wasn't a question; it was a statement.

"Yeah, she did," I murmur apologetically.

"Of course, she did." He takes his spot back on the couch and resumes staring at the TV. I lie back in the recliner and snuggle up against Adam. He wraps his arm around me, planting a kiss on my forehead. I really wish my brother and my best friend would figure out their crap and get it solved.

"You're back!" I yell out when I see Alexis. My first thought was oh no when I saw her wearing Brad's clothes. It wasn't because I was upset that she did it, it was because I was afraid of Ethan's reaction. I give her a hug and ask the obvious question. "So, how was it?" Out of the corner of my eye, I see Ethan get up and walk out. Alexis shoots off the couch and runs after him.

I let out a heavy sigh and curl up next to Adam again.

### Alexis

The whole time I am getting ready, my body is shaking; my stomach is full of nerves. He is here, though part of me wishes he wasn't. The only reason he is here is for Kaylee, not me. More than anything, I wish he were here for me. I want Ethan to be my date for the prom. I want Ethan to be who I dance with tonight. Ethan, not Brad. Brad is wonderful and sweet. Yes, I feel for him too, but not the way I do for Ethan. Ethan owns me, all of me. I feel guilty for wanting two guys, even though my want for one outweighs the other. If only the one I really wanted, wanted me in return.

Brad walks up to me and tells me how beautiful I look. My insides flip in response. I don't dare look at Ethan. I know he is watching us since I can feel the heat of his gaze. Brad shakily slips on my corsage. The flowers are pink like my dress. My dress is a brighter pink that stops just above my knees. It is strapless and has the sweetheart top. I matched it with my four-inch silver heels.

Out of the corner of my eye, I see him. He tells Kaylee, his sister, that she is beautiful. What he says next makes my heart leap with hope. "Both of you do." I try to stay composed when he kisses me on the cheek. I smile faintly at him, trying to look unaffected.

Needing to get out of here, I say good-bye to Anna and Jack and let Brad walk me out. He opens the door to his white Chevy Silverado for me. I notice Ethan standing on the porch, staring at me intently.

"You ready?" Brad asks breaking the staring match Ethan and I are having.

I decide right then that I am going to have fun tonight and not let Ethan get to me. If he wants me, he should say so. As far as I'm concerned, it's his loss. "Hell, yeah!" I smile brightly at Brad as he puts the truck in reverse and backs out of the driveway.

We get at least two miles down the road before my phone chimes with a message.

**Ethan: Have fun tonight and be careful. Let me know when you make it home so I know you're safe. If you need me to come get you all you have to do is call. If he touches you, I'll kill him.**

See! This is what I mean! Ethan acts like wants me, but he won't do anything about it! Guys talk about how girls are so confusing, but hello, guys have no room to talk!

**Me: I will have fun tonight, don't worry ;) I'm sure I won't need you so don't wait up. Whatever happens, happens!**

I press send and immediately wish I hadn't. I shouldn't have said any of that to him. Yes, I will have fun, but Brad and I will not go as far as having sex tonight. We might kiss, but nothing more.

I anxiously wait for him to reply. Brad starts to make conversation with me so I answer him while I occasionally check my phone for a reply from Ethan.

After we eat dinner, we head to the country club that is hosting the prom. There is still no reply from Ethan when we arrive so I turn my phone off. I know if I leave it on, I'll keep constantly checking it throughout the night. It is rude for me to be on a date with Brad and check my phone constantly for messages from Ethan.

I link my arm through Brad's and let him lead me inside. We pause, letting them take our picture at the door. Our theme this year was "A Night in Paris." There is an Eiffel Tower hovering over the senior lead-out platform. The decorations are enchanting. Globes with soft lighting hang from the ceiling to accent the theme.

"Would you like something to drink?" Brad asks.

"Yes, please." I watch him as he walks over to the drink table and pours me a drink. Brad is always courteous, always smiling. No one really has a bad thing to say about him. He is the type of friend who will come running the moment you need him and he never complains when you ask him for help. Brad is tall and lean with a little bit of muscle. At five-foot-ten, he is just a few inches taller than me. His short sandy blond hair is combed to the right side. His hazel eyes will stand out in any crowd.

He returns with my drink and I sip on it while we mingle with some of our friends. Most girls here are wearing beautiful evening gowns while some, like me, are wearing shorter dresses that stop mid-thigh.

"Would you like to dance?" He holds out his hand, inviting me to the dance floor. Nodding, I take it and let him lead me. When we find a spot on the dance floor, he surprises me by spinning me around and then tugs me to him. With one hand firm around my waist and the other grasping my hand, we dance to the soft, passionate beat of the music. If I weren't so hung up on Ethan, I would seriously consider dating Brad. Brad is the essence of a good guy, one of the very few guys who are loyal to their girl.

He stares deep into my eyes as we keep moving to the rhythm of the song. Every now and then, he twirls me around, but he never once takes his eyes off mine.

The only time we aren't together tonight is when we parted for a few minutes to socialize. Even then, I found myself searching for him like I couldn't stand to be away from him.

We leave prom around ten o'clock and go to an after party held at a football player's house. Ted, I think. I still keep my phone turned off so I wouldn't be tempted to look at it. The truth is that I am having so much fun with Brad it's keeping my mind off Ethan.

On the makeshift dance floor, I grind against Brad like it is nobody's business. I miss having Kaylee as my wingman, but Brad is filling the position quite nicely. We drink and talk about little things. The more I get to know Brad, the more I like, which is causing a problem for me. I am crushing on two guys and I'm not sure who I want more.

Brad and I have just finished dancing when he asks, "You want go back to my place? My parents are gone for the night."

My eyebrow arches up at his question wondering if he is suggesting what I think he is. He notices my reaction and immediately adds, "I didn't mean that, unless you wanted to, of course," he says with a smirk. "I just meant we could hang out and watch a movie or something."

"Sure. I'm up for that," I answer honestly. I am glad he asked because I am not ready for the night to end. He grins widely and leads me out to his truck, away from the party.

*Alexis*

*"I had to have one last look at her before I'm locked away in my own personal hell, for good."-*
*Riley*

Brad offers me a pair of his shorts and a t-shirt to change into while we watch the movie. The shorts hang loosely around my waist and the shirt completely swallows me, but I feel comfortable. When I walk back into the living room, Brad has already changed. My eyes rake over his bare chest for a split second before I avert my eyes. I really don't want him to catch me staring.

I stretch out on the couch as the movie starts. Brad walks in with a big bowl of popcorn and two beers. After setting the food on the coffee table and handing me my beer, he grabs a blanket from the recliner and plops down on the couch next to me before covering me up.

Halfway through the movie, two beers, and a bowl of popcorn, we ended up laying long ways on the couch with him behind me, my back to his front. His arm wraps around my middle keeping me close to him. My insides melt at the warmth of his touch.

We stay like that until the credits roll. I suck in a breath when his hot breath tickles my neck. Goosebumps break out over my body when he nibbles on my neck. He nudges me back so I turn until I am facing him. My mouth immediately goes to his for a hungry kiss. With his hand on my neck, his thumb strokes my cheek as his tongue caresses mine.

The way I'm feeling at this moment, I want to say to hell with it and surrender to him, but there is a voice in the back of my head saying I need to stop. I didn't want to listen to it, though I know it is right.

Placing my hand on his chest, I push him back slightly. "Brad..." I pant.

He doesn't seem frustrated or regretful; his eyes still burn with hunger. "It's okay," he whispers, tucking a strand of hair behind my ear. "It wasn't my intention to go any farther but don't expect me to say I'm sorry or I regret it because I don't."

I swallow against the lump in my throat. "I would hope not," I reply, still breathless. He smiles before picking up where we were before I stopped him. Should I still be dating Brad when I'm hung up on Ethan? No, it isn't fair to Brad. Being drawn to a guy who likes to play with your emotions sucks.

I bury my head in the crook of Brad's neck and close my eyes. With every breath, his cologne fills my lungs, igniting my senses. He kisses my forehead as I drift off to sleep, not acting on my current craving.

The weight of a body has me pinned to the couch when I awake. Brad's head is nestled on my chest with his leg thrown over mine. *I can't believe I stayed the night.* Trying to wrestle my way out of Brad's arms turns out to be harder than I thought. Every time I move, his arms tighten around me. I sigh and settle for waking him up. "Brad, wake up." I shake him lightly. After a minute, he stirs and rubs his eyes. "I need to get going. I'm sure Kaylee is freaking out because I haven't checked in." Ethan too, but I don't say it.

He releases me and I turn on my phone, planning to call Kaylee. Shit! It's almost noon! I quickly dial Kaylee's number, letting her know where I am, and that I am okay. As I feared, she had been worried. I promised to call her later and fill her in on my night with Brad. I hang up and check my messages. The messaging app opens and all of them are from Ethan.

*Where are you?*

*Are you okay?*

*Please let me know if you're okay.*

*Alexis, please call me, I'm worried about you*

Crap! What have I done?

Brad's voice breaks me out of my reverie. "Are you sure you have to go? We can hang out for the day and I'll take you home tonight." As much as I want to, I don't think it is a good idea.

"I sort of promised Kaylee I'd spend the day with her." I let the lie roll off my tongue easily. It is partly true since I plan on seeing her for a little while today. We just never made plans to. I feel guilty for lying, but I need time to think about what I want and I can't do that if I am around him all day.

I attempt to fix my bed hair and pick up my dress.

"Okay." He throws a shirt on, puts his University of Kentucky hat on, grabs his keys, and follows me out.

Panic threads my body when I realize I will show up at Kaylee's in Brad's clothes. *Please don't let Ethan be there.*

My panic hadn't settled by the time that we arrived; it got worse. Sure enough, sitting in the driveway at Adam's is Ethan's truck. Brad must've noticed my unease because he grasps my hand comfortingly. "I had a great time last night."

"I did too," I reply honestly because I did.

"I'll see you tomorrow, babe."

"Okay."

He smiles brightly before kissing the back of my hand. I let him open the door for me and walk me to the door. "Oh, I need to give you your clothes back."

Brad shakes his head. "No, you keep them." He kisses my cheek then my mouth once before leaving. After taking a deep breath, I turn the knob and step inside.

I find Kaylee sitting in the recliner eating ramen noodles. Adam is beside her watching TV. "You're back!" Kaylee exclaims excitedly. I walk in further and my stomach plummets. As I figured, Ethan is occupying the couch. He snaps his head in my direction at Kaylee's announcement of my arrival. She gets up from the recliner and gives me a hug. Ethan looks away and focuses his attention on the TV. He is pissed. I know exactly what is running through his mind right now. "So, how was it?" Kaylee wiggled her eyebrows. There could be two meanings to that question. If I know my best friend, I know which question she is really asking.

Ethan shoots up from the couch and walks out before I answer her. Leaving Kaylee hanging, I chase after Ethan. "Ethan, wait!" I holler after him. He stops abruptly but doesn't turn to face me. "Nothing happened." I answer his unspoken question, cutting right to the chase. I know why he walked out; I'm not stupid.

"It's not of my business if you did. We aren't together. If you want to have sex with him, then do it." His voice is ice cold.

"Why are you acting this way?" I murmur.

He spins around and glares at me. "Why? I don't hear from you all night and you show up wearing his clothes. All night I worried about you, wondering if you were okay. My mind was conjuring up things that could've happened to you! Things I would kill someone for if they ever did that to you!" He stops to collect himself. "When you walked in wearing that, I was hurt. I wasn't about to sit in there and listen to you gush over how wonderful your night was with another guy, I couldn't bear it." He thrusts his hands into his hair and scrubs his face in frustration.

Not knowing what else to say, I murmur, "I'm sorry."

We are quiet for a long moment before he turns and walks away. I let him go so he can calm down and maybe we can sort things out later. Hopefully, things will work out with us because he is who I really want.

*Kaylee*

*"Staring at these four walls is driving me crazy since all I do is think about her. I think about her smile, her laugh, and what I did."- Riley*

Surprisingly, the house sold quickly; it was only on the market for two weeks. The cars sold last week so now that all of that is over with, I need to pay my mother a visit. The same mother who blames me for Dad's death. The same mother who is now in jail because she covered Riley's ass and tried to get my father's money from me. I'm actually looking forward to this visit. Nothing she says will hurt me like it used to because, for once, I came out on top. For once, I don't feel sad or broken. I feel relieved that everything has come full circle.

Ethan and I paid another visit to Dad the other day to thank him. I thanked him for being such a wonderful father and loving me unconditionally, and I thanked him for the things he left me. The money, the house, the cars…I don't deserve any of it.

Ugh! Seriously! These pants just fit me a few days ago! I mean they button, but it digs into my skin because they are so tight. To say that I've been hormonal is an understatement. I will cry for no reason and get mad at the stupidest things. Poor Adam has been so patient with me through my mood swings. Not to mention that my boobs have been sore, which Adam likes because they are bigger than normal.

There is a slight knock on the door before Adam sticks his head in. "You ready?"

I flop down on the bed defeated. "My pants don't fit anymore."

He chuckles and sits beside me, sliding his arm around me. "What do you expect, sweetheart? You're pregnant." He kisses my temple then settles his hand on my belly. It looks like I've gained at least ten pounds!

"That doesn't make me feel better," I grumble.

"You are still beautiful, Kaylee. I swear you could wear anything and still be gorgeous. Your hair could be in a mess, wearing no make-up and sweatpants, and you'd still be beautiful." I blush from his comment. He always knows what to say to make me smile.

"How about I let you borrow a pair of my sweats, and then after you talk to Elizabeth, we will go get you some that do fit?"

"Okay."

Adam and I walk hand in hand behind the officer that leads us back to where people usually visit with the inmates. An unnerving feeling enters my body so I walk closer beside Adam. He lets go of my hand and wraps his arm protectively around me, which helps the creeped out feeling I have. And to think I thought about going alone?

Adam and I sit down and wait for them to bring her out. Adam places his hand on my thigh letting his thumb stroke the inside of my leg. "I love you," he mouths before leaning in to kiss me. His lips barely touch mine when we hear a snort. I turn and come face to face with my mother. God, she looks awful. Her hair looks greasy, probably because she doesn't have her expensive hair products, and her face looks pale without all of her make-up. She is in an orange jumpsuit with handcuffs on her wrists.

"Is there a problem?" I retort.

"Besides the fact that you made me lose my job, ruined my social life, and had unnecessary charges filed against me, no. It means you've done more than enough already." She sits how she normally does, all prim and proper.

"I believe you have yourself to thank for that. All I did was try to stay away from you as much as possible. I hardly asked you for anything nor did I expect anything other than what a mother should provide for their child. I didn't think it was too much to ask for since you are my mother or rather was." She scoffs like she is offended. "Not to mention the fact that you tried to kill me and my best friend!"

"And what exactly did you expect from me?" she asks, ignoring my last comment.

"Love. I expected you to love me unconditionally especially when I needed you the most. If it weren't for Dad, I wouldn't have known what it felt like to have a parent who loved their child. A mother is supposed provide for their child. You hardly kept food in the house and you acted like it was a crime when I asked you for money so I could eat at school. Why was it so hard to love me?"

She laughs bitterly. "Because, as I've repeated to you on various occasions, you ruined my life. It was your fault that your father and I never got along. You got in the way of our relationship. He loved you so much that I knew I wouldn't be important to him anymore. So I decided I wanted an abortion, hoping we could rekindle the love that we'd lost. He threatened to divorce me and leave me with nothing if I went through with it! I was so envious of you! You stole all of his attention, his time, and his love! So I have every right to blame you!" She sat there emotionless. I'm not going to take the blame she is throwing my way. Dad was only doing what a parent does.

"See, that's where you're wrong. Dad was doing what he was supposed to. The problems you and Dad had obviously started way before I came into the picture. When I first found out I was pregnant, I was horrified. Not only was I horrified because I thought I was going to lose Adam, but I wasn't sure I could be a mom since the only mother figure I had hated my guts. I thought you had hated me because of what happened to Dad. I spent years blaming myself and barely living, all because you made me believe that I was selfish for dragging Dad out.

"Because of you, I was blind to who Riley really was. My first relationship was with an abusive jock who took my innocence. He never cared for me. I was just another conquest to him though at the time I didn't see it. Maybe I just wanted to believe I was worth something to somebody. Sure, I had Alexis, but I wanted a relationship with a guy instead of thinking I'd be alone for the rest of my life. I just wanted to be wanted. With Adam, I have all of that. He has shown me what love really is. The fact that he is willing to take responsibility for someone who wasn't planned proves that. I wouldn't want it any other way. Yes, I wish they were his, but regardless, I know he will be there and love them as they are. This might sound crazy, but if I had a chance to do it all over again, I wouldn't change a thing. That may sound heartless since I would lose my father again, but he would understand since he knows unconditional love."

She sits there seeming unaffected by anything I just shared. "They? Are you having twins?" When I nod, she laughs humorlessly. "So you think since you found 'true love,' as you put it, it will make you a good mother?" She uses her fingers to make air quotations.

"Well, I think that it is a good possibility since you've shown me how not to act."

"You made me that way, remember?"

Adam speaks up before I can reply. "Can you go two seconds without trying to tear her down? I'm so damn proud of her for handling everything the way she has. She is so strong despite what she has had to deal with. I'm tired of you blaming her for your problems. Will you ever grow up and think of anyone besides yourself? How Kaylee didn't succumb to your selfish ways amazes me, but I'm so glad she didn't. I hope you rot in hell for torturing her." Adam says all of that as calm as can be.

I half expect her to be pissed, but no, she grins from ear to ear. Adam just told her to go to hell and she is smiling like he gave her a compliment? Good Lord, she is crazy! I pat his leg appreciatively.

"If you two are done spouting off nonsense, then I would like for you to leave." Her eyes narrow at me when I let out a snort.

"Actually, there is a reason for my visit." I grin widely. "I really hope you're not planning on getting out anytime soon."

"You thought I'd be here long? That's rich."

"I figured you'd try to find a way to weasel your way out. That makes this all that much more amusing."

"You act like you're so high and mighty all of a sudden," she says sarcastically.

"You would be too if you just inherited a ton of money." Fear flashes in her eyes for a moment. "I mean, I did just sell a house and two cars and not to mention half of the money that you so greedily kept to yourself. Of course, you don't get the other half…that goes to Ethan." I almost wanted to laugh in her face, but I'm not that much of a bitch. I think by leaving her with nothing is good enough. "So, you see, either way you end up with nothing. How does it feel? It sucks, doesn't it?" Her body starts violently shaking with rage, and her eyes look murderous.

Adam must have sensed what she was about to do because he grabbed me and jerked me out of the way from her launching herself at me. Two officers who are standing by quickly tackle her to the ground. "You bitch! You will pay for this! How could you do this to me after everything I did for you!"

I just roll my eyes and leave.

You know what's so great about karma? It does all of the dirty work for you. My mother thought she had broken me completely. Little did she know she actually ruined herself instead of me. Yeah, I was a little broken, but not entirely. As they say, karma is a bitch. Mom...well, Elizabeth actually, got it served on a silver platter without a fork. I don't feel remorse for leaving her with nothing. The way I see it, she has a bed and she gets three meals a day. Plus, I think orange suits her well. It always was her color.

Life has a way of making a complete one eighty without acknowledging you first. It could be your saving grace or your worst enemy. It has been both for me. More importantly, it taught me how to be strong when I want to be weak.

## 29

*Kaylee*

*"Remind me again why I like shopping?"- Kaylee*

"Oh, look how cute this is!" Anna holds up an infant dress for me to see. It is black and has pink flowers on it.

"That's adorable!" I take it from her and add it to the cart. I'm trying hard to be responsible and stay on a budget, but seeing all these cute clothes makes it tough, especially since I have to buy for two babies.

Anna, Alexis, and I are out getting everything we need for Jasmine and Jackson. We are planning to get everything in one trip so we won't be rushed to get everything ready for their arrival in a little over two months. Adam, Jack, and Ethan are getting all of the furniture and are supposed to put some of it together today. So far, we have bought all the things they need except for the bedding, diapers, and a few more clothes.

Two hours later, we leave the store with everything we set out to buy plus extra stuff we just couldn't pass up. My feet and legs are screaming at me for being on my feet for so long.

The babies and I decide we want some ice cream so we stop at the frozen yogurt place downtown. When we all have our orders, we pick a booth and sit down.

"Are you getting excited, sweetie?" Anna asks.

"I think I'm more nervous than anything." From the stories I've heard, labor sounds scary.

"It's normal to feel that way. Don't worry; Adam will be there to help you through it. Me too, if you need me." She gives me a reassuring smile and clasps my hand.

We are interrupted by a woman shouting.

"It's not fair!" the woman screeches.

I turn my head in the direction I hear the woman yelling to see what is going on and I immediately wish I hadn't.

"No, George! I'm not going to let this go any longer!" Riley's mother, Cynthia, yells, causing everyone in the building to focus their attention on her and me. This is not good. She makes a beeline for our table, her eyes burning with rage.

She thrusts her finger in my direction. "You! How could you do this to him, to his future?! He had everything going for him! You destroyed his life with your pretentious lies!" she bellows at me angrily.

I stand up from my seat, keeping a safe distance. "Why do you still believe that he is innocent? I'm sorry that your son turned out to be an abusive asshole, but I'm not sorry for finally turning him in! It's his fault his future is ruined. He made his choices, Cynthia, and now he has to live with what he did!"

Her eyes widen when she takes in my rounded stomach. At twenty-six weeks pregnant, it's definitely noticeable. "Is it his?" My mouth forms a firm line at her question.

Hearing her call my babies 'it' only infuriates me more. "He was always impatient and kept pressuring me to have sex with him, but I didn't. That night he took the one thing that was special to me and brutally stripped it from me. Riley may have gotten me pregnant, but he is not the father." I place my hand protectively on my growing belly. "Riley will not be anywhere near my kids. I will not put them through the hurt and suffering I went through."

Cynthia's veins throb erratically in her throat. "You can't keep his child from him! He deserves to be in their life!"

"Are you crazy? My children are not going anywhere near him!"

"Why do you keep saying children? Are planning on having more than one with him?" George, Riley's dad, raises his eyebrow questioningly.

"Hell, no! If I ever have any more kids, it will be with Adam. Since you obviously haven't figured it out, I'm having twins. Now if you will excuse me, I have to get home to Adam, who is the babies' father." I sneer at their shocked looks. Turning around, I grab my yogurt and my purse before brushing past Cynthia and George.

I am almost out the door when Cynthia says something that stops me in my tracks. "Don't think this is over, Kaylee. You can't keep his children from him! Enjoy them while you can because as soon they are born, I'm getting custody of them and you will never see them again!"

She can't do that, can she?

I make my feet carry me to Anna's car and get in. I sigh in relief when I close the car door, but it doesn't stop the tears that prick my eyes or the panic that is settling in my chest. My arms hug my belly the whole ride home.

"Sweetie, please don't stress over what she said. She has nothing against you that says you are a bad mother. She can't take them from you, I promise." Smiling faintly, she squeezes my hand reassuringly. In my heart, I know she is right, but doubts fill my head. "Stress is not good for the babies. Please don't worry about it." I nod slowly, still reeling from Cynthia's threat.

"Come on, baby girl, let's get you inside so you can rest. You've had a long day." Alexis helps me from the car and into the house.

I snuggle Adam's pillow, wishing he were here. No sooner than my head hit the pillow, I am out.

*Adam*

The first thing I do when I notice the girls are home is go see my girl. I find her asleep, snuggling my pillow with a frown etched on her face. I give her a quick kiss on the forehead and pull the covers up to her neck before helping unload the truck.

When the truck is unloaded, I head to the kitchen to help Mom and Alexis put away everything. Mainly, I want to see what they got. I stop suddenly when I hear them talking.

"You don't really think that Cynthia has the power to do that…does she? I mean why is she dead set on believing her son is innocent? Why would she want the babies subjected to that?" Alexis asked, worry echoed in her voice.

"Alexis, honey, it doesn't matter if they have all the money in the world or the best lawyer in the world, they will not get custody of our grandchildren. I don't think she really wants them, to be honest. I think she is just trying to scare Kaylee into letting Riley be in their lives," Mom assures her.

Having heard enough, I round the corner. "He is not going to be anywhere near Kaylee or my kids and no one is going to take them from me. I will make sure of it," I vow.

Surprise plasters their faces when they realize I had been listening.

I turn back around and stalk back up to my room where my girl is sleeping. Slipping under the covers, I pull her to me, kissing her temple. The frown she wore curls into a smile as she wraps her loving arms around my waist.

I stay awake, watching her sleep in my arms. I haven't done this in a while. Taking in every breath, every sigh, every movement she makes, I reminisce back to the night that changed everything for us. Her beat-up car brought us together and Riley, as painful as it is to admit, also had a hand in bringing us together. With every hurtful word and every heartbreaking hit, she would inch closer to me. How awful does it sound that I'm practically thanking him for what he did? Does that make me crazy? Probably. I hate what he did to her, I want to kill him slowly, make him suffer like she did, but what Kaylee said makes sense. Her life led her to this moment after taking a tragic turn for the worst. If she would endure all of that again so she could be with me, then maybe thanking Riley for pushing her to me doesn't sound crazy at all. She is willing to suffer from losing her father, who she loved more than life, and take every damaging hit that Riley thrust at her to be happy with me and our expecting twins. God, I love this girl so much. She is so strong despite the things she's endured. She almost died…three times in the last five years. My heart drops and my chest aches just thinking about it.

From this day forward, I'm going to do everything I can to make sure that I protect her, Jasmine, and Jackson. I will love them and cherish them forever. When I take my last breath, I will use it by telling them I love them more than life.

Who knows where our lives will take us or what we will endure. Things happen; it's a part of life. But that doesn't mean that I'm not going to do everything I can to protect them from it.

Kaylee stirs, interrupting my thoughts. "How are you feeling, sweetheart?" Her eyes flutter open for a moment then close again. I caress her cheek with the back of my fingers.

"Exhausted and hungry," she replies still half asleep. "I think I overdid it today because my feet are killing me," she adds with a groan.

"How about I get you something to eat, and while you eat, I will massage your feet." Her eyes blinked a couple of times like she couldn't believe what I just said.

"That would feel amazing," she finally says. Her beautiful blue eyes capture mine as I lower my head to kiss her. Cradling her head, I devour her mouth until her stomach decides to growl breaking the spell.

I bark out a laugh and kiss her one more time before heading into the kitchen.

As promised, when I return with her food, I start massaging her feet. "You know your ankles are swollen?"

She looks down at her feet. "Ugh, really?"

"I'm going to go get some ice for them. I'll be right back."

When I return, I place the ice on both of her ankles and elevate them using a pillow.

My eyes drift up to Kaylee, noticing she is too quiet. She is staring off into space, a frown on her face. "What are you thinking so hard about, sweetheart?"

She snaps out of it and looks at me, her eyes full of sadness. "I saw Riley's parents earlier. Cynthia was yelling at me, causing a scene about how I ruined his future with all my 'lies.' She thinks our babies should be in his life. I told her that he wasn't getting anywhere near them and that you are the twins' father. She claims she is going to get custody of them the day they are born." Her eyes and her hands drop to her well-rounded stomach. We have roughly fourteen weeks left until we get to meet Jackson and Jasmine. I'll be damned if they try to take them from us.

I move on the bed and sit next to her, placing my hands on top of hers. "Kaylee, look at me, sweetheart. No one will take them away from us, I swear. She is just talking a bunch of nonsense." Leaning forward, I brush my lips against hers, devouring the softness of her mouth. "I love you, Kaylee Harper, and I can't wait to meet our son and daughter." I draw back, resting my forehead on hers so I can gaze into her breathtaking blue eyes.

She withdraws her hands from her belly, bringing them up to my face. "There are times when I think I can't possibly love you more, and each time you prove me wrong. I love you more than life, Adam. I thank God every day for bringing you to me because without you, I wouldn't know what it feels like to be loved again."

"Get used to it, sweetheart, because I will never stop showing you how much I love you."

## Adam

*"I think I always knew a spot would be reserved for me in hell."- Riley*

I'm nervous as hell. My palms are sweating, I keep checking the time on my phone every two minutes, fidgeting…you name it; I'm doing it. Kaylee and I are going out tonight, just the two of us. Normally, I wouldn't be this nervous to go on a date with her, but tonight I have a surprise, a big one. I've been planning this for a while now. After checking and double-checking every detail to make sure things are in order, I finally get dressed.

Ethan slaps me on the back. "Dude, calm down, she will love it." I can't speak so I just nod.

"Bro, listen to me. You have nothing to worry about. She loves you. Now stop! Just think how surprised she will be," Brad adds. Taking a deep breath, I pat my pockets, making sure I have everything.

Dad walks up and gives me a hug. "Normally, I wouldn't agree to this since you are only eighteen and you just graduated, but what you and Kaylee have is far more than what most married couples do. Anyone can look at you both and see it. They're right son; don't worry. Relax."

"Thanks, Dad. Love you."

"And I love you."

Brad grabs me by my shoulders and shakes me. "For the last time, Adam, calm the hell down. If she sees you acting like this, she'll know something's up."

"Yeah, dude, the surprise will be ruined the moment she sees you if you don't quit!" Ethan lightly slaps my face a couple of times.

Straightening my shirt, I go over the plans one last time. I'm taking her to dinner, to see a show, and finally a walk in the park down the street from the house.

My heart races at the sound of feet walking down the hall. When she walks into view, the air suddenly leaves my lungs. Her smile is bright and beautiful. Kaylee is wearing a spaghetti strap, yellow sundress that shows off her well-rounded stomach. Her hair pulled back into a braided bun.

Her beauty leaves me so stunned that I didn't know my mouth had been hanging open until someone's hand pushes my jaw upward. Her cheeks flame red as she laughs at my expression.

Closing the gap between us, I reach out, taking her hand, and pull her to me. Her body melts into mine perfectly like always. I tilt her head up and kiss her passionately. "I love you," I murmur.

"I love you, too." All the nerves leave me at her words.

We say good-bye and take off for our first destination. Dinner. I let her choose the place since her cravings have been all over the place lately. She chooses a nice Italian restaurant in the middle of town. It is quiet, intimate and, of course, not expensive. It wouldn't have mattered to me if she chose the most expensive restaurant. As long as I was with her, we could go anywhere and I'd be the happiest guy in the world.

After dinner, we head to the show I planned for us to see. We take our seats in the middle section. Kaylee still has no idea what we are seeing yet. She keeps asking me, but I just smile and shake my head. She'll find out soon enough.

When the lights dim and the show starts, I watch for her reaction. The precise moment she realizes what kind of show it is, her jaw drops and her eyes glisten with tears.

I heard about a dance showcase taking place and I knew I had to bring her knowing how much she loved and missed it. Sliding my hand into hers, I lift it up and brush my lips against the back of her hand.

My eyes barely glance toward the stage the whole two hours. I focus intently on Kaylee, and how every memory flickers in her eyes. She is so lost in the show; it's like a little kid seeing something magical.

When the show is over, my nerves start to come back slowly. It's almost time for my last surprise, and it's the big one.

"Adam," she whispers when we step outside. She eagerly wraps her arms around me. "I love you. Thank you for everything." I wipe away the lone tear that is sliding down her cheek.

"Anything for you, sweetheart," I whisper against her sweet, soft lips. "Are you ready for your last surprise?" I lead her back to the truck when she nods.

Before she gets in, I blindfold her so she can't see it as soon as we pull up. Otherwise, it will ruin the surprise.

When we reach our destination, I help her out and lead her down the familiar path through the park. As usual, she keeps asking me what we are doing. I just laugh and tell her that she'll find out soon enough.

We slow to a stop when I finally reach the concrete slab. "You ready, sweetheart?" I whisper in her ear. She shakily nods. My hands tremble trying to remove the blindfold from her eyes.

Kaylee's hand flies to her mouth and she gasps when she sees the decorated basketball court. Her eyes twinkle from the candles that are lit, which spell out 'I love you' with basketballs as the 'o' in love and you. Purple rose petals outline the words, forming the shape of a heart. Lights drape from each rim, connecting in the middle.

She turns to face me and smiles. "How did…when?"

Grabbing her hand, I walk her onto the court. "I had some help." I shrug and leave it at that.

"It's so beautiful, Adam!" she exclaims happily.

"Like you." Clasping the box in my left pocket, I take a slow, deep breath and drop to one knee. My eyes never leave hers as I pull out the velvet box and open it. "Kaylee, you have made me the happiest man alive. I want nothing more than to spend the rest of my life with you, Jackson, and Jasmine. You three are my life, now and forever. Will you marry me?" My thumb strokes the back of her hand nervously.

"Oh, Adam. Yes!" Standing up, I slide the ring on her finger and slam my mouth to hers. My left hand caresses her belly as I kiss her slowly, more thoroughly.

"Dance with me?" When she says yes, I walk over and plug my iPod into the stereo of my truck. The first song, *Let's Don't Call It a Night* by Casey James, says it all.

She walks into my waiting arms and lays her head against my chest. I didn't think I could be any happier than when we finally were together. Boy was I wrong. Right now, this is the happiest moment of my life. I know that the next one will be even better than this one.

The song changes to Bruno Mars' *Just the Way You Are*, and I know that this song is perfect for her. I played this one for her the day at the gym and I know I will play it for her again one day.

I twirl, dip, and kiss her throughout each song until it is time to go. I would stay out here all night dancing with her if I wasn't afraid she would overdo it.

*Kaylee*

The next couple of months goes by in a whirlwind. With graduation and getting ready for the twins, who seem to want to take their sweet time coming, the days go by fairly quickly, though not soon enough. I was finally glad when graduation came and went. I was so afraid I'd fall while walking up the steps to receive my diploma, so I took my time. If it were up to me, I would've skipped it, but everyone wanted to see me waddle across the stage with my almost eight-month pregnant belly sticking out. By the time the ceremony was over, I was more than ready for a nap.

The guest bedroom transformed into the nursery until Adam and I get our own place. We have sort of started looking, but nothing has caught our attention yet. Right now, we aren't in a hurry since we decided to stay at least until after Jasmine and Jackson are born. Anna and Alexis have been planning the wedding nonstop since the morning after Adam proposed. Most girls would be upset with the fact that the guy asked while she was pregnant. In their mind, they think that the only reason they asked was because she was pregnant. With Adam, I knew that wasn't true. He asked because he loves me. Adam didn't ask just because it was 'the right thing to do.' There was no doubt in my mind that his love for me ran deep and vice versa. That night was beyond perfect. It was better than I could've ever imagined.

We decide to get married on October tenth, the anniversary of my father's death. My life changed forever on that day and it will forever change again when I officially become Mrs. Lucas Adam Thomas. Change happens every day in some shape or form. Most of the time, we are too busy to notice it. Change can be wonderful, but it can also be heartbreaking. I've experienced both and yet I wouldn't trade or give away any day of my life. Yeah, I miss my father, but I've come to the realization that he never really left. He is always with me and will be forever. My life had been a fairy tale that turned into a nightmare before turning back into everything I'd dreamed and hoped it would be. I have the family I'd always wanted. Blood doesn't make a family. I never believed that until I experienced it myself.

If I have ever made fun of a pregnant woman, I'm certainly paying for it now. Oh my God, I'm dying, literally. It is so hot outside today. Alexis wanted to go for a swim in the humongous pool she has. Normally, I wouldn't mind, but the heat is really scorching today and I don't have the energy to get up, so I just lounge in the shade.

When I can't stand it anymore, I sit up and start making my way inside. "I'm starving. Let's get something to eat," I holler at her over my shoulder.

Adam is helping his dad in the shop today, spending some time with him. He is still adamant about me not working at all. I told him I'd think about it. However, I still don't know if I could stay home. The babies would keep me busy, but there is the whole issue of me wanting to help support our little family. Maybe I will get used to it, maybe not. Who knows? Maybe after I start working, I'll find I won't like it. I keep telling myself that if I don't work, it doesn't mean that I'm mooching off anyone. Try telling that to the other part of me that's being unreasonable.

"What you want to eat?" Alexis asks while raiding the cabinets.

"Ice cream," I say with a laugh. I swear that throughout this pregnancy I've eaten a ton of ice cream. It seems to be what the little ones want the most of.

She just laughs and shakes her head. "That's not surprising."

I shrug and wait patiently for her to scoop some of my favorite cookie dough ice cream into a bowl for me.

When she sets it in front of me, I smile thankfully and dig in. "How are things with Brad?" Her eyes sparkle a little before it fades just a tad.

"Things are great actually," she replies with a genuine smile. "He is amazingly sweet. Did I tell you he told me that he loved me?"

"What? No way! When?"

"The night he asked me to prom."

"Wow. What did you say? Do you honestly love him?" I don't think she really does love Brad.

"I haven't told him. I could see myself loving him…"

My brow rises questioningly. "I feel a 'but' coming on."

"But, I don't know if he is the one for me."

"Why do you say that?"

She sighs, staring at her bowl of ice cream. "There isn't enough spark between us. He isn't a bad kisser, I just want more."

I don't know exactly how to answer that since I haven't felt that way. Adam makes me melt when he kisses me. "How do you feel about Ethan?"

She looks up from her bowl of ice cream, a smile trying to break free. "Just being in the same room as him makes me feel things I have never felt before. Sparks fly when he smiles, and my heart practically beats out of my chest when his eyes penetrate mine."

Wow, that's pretty deep. "It sounds like you have it bad. Why are you with Brad then if Ethan is who you really want?"

"I like them both. Brad seems safer. I don't see him breaking my heart like Ethan."

"Don't choose Brad just because you think you will be happy, Alexis. You will only end up hurting not only you but also him in the process."

She smiles faintly while finishing off what was left of her ice cream. "No matter who I choose, someone will get hurt. I honestly like Brad. I just can't see myself being with him like I can Ethan."

"I know it sucks, but the longer you string Brad along, the more hurt he will be. Ethan needs to get his head on straight before he loses you for good. If he really wants to be with you, he will." I smile supportively. "Now, what movie do you want to watch?"

## 31

*Kaylee*

*"Why is love so complicated?"- Alexis*

A sharp pain in my stomach wakes me in the night. I'm lying on my side, my back to Adam, with his protective arm around my waist. I breathe deeply, riding it out.

At our previous doctor appointment a week ago, I was dilated to one so we were expecting them to come soon. Maybe not today. I want them out, yet at the same time, I'm scared. Will I make a good mother? Will I automatically know what to do? My mind is running with scary thoughts, which in turn freak me out.

I flinch, squeezing my eyes shut as I ride out another contraction. Anxiety and fear spread through me, forming a lump in my throat.

My hand grips Adam's at the next one. If I'm timing them correctly, they are about ten minutes apart. These are worse than the others I have had.

"Kaylee, are you okay, sweetheart?" Adam asks groggily. Shaking my head in response, I swallow against the lump unable to answer him. I know if I tell him I'm not okay, he will worry. "Are you hurting?" More awake now, he leaps from the bed and turns the light on before kneeling in front of me. I don't answer him because I'm not sure.

Anxiety is building, my breaths are becoming quicker, and I'm starting to sweat. I'm on the verge of panicking. "Breathe, Kaylee. You can do this, just breathe." Oh Adam, you always know what to say. His hand massages my back while I have the other one locked tight in my grip. "I'm going to wake Mom up and then we are going to take you to the hospital, okay? I'll just be two seconds then I'll be right back. Relax and continue to breathe. Can you do that for me?" I shakily nod before reluctantly letting his hand go. How is he so calm right now? I'm on the verge of hyperventilating.

He was back as soon as he was gone like he promised. He throws on some clothes, grabs my bag and both diaper bags before holding out his hand to help me stand.

With one arm around my waist, he walks me out. I have to stop a couple of times because the pain is too much.

When we pull up at the hospital, Adam immediately hops out, but I am frozen, I can't move. "Come on, sweetheart." He holds out his hand, but I don't take it. My arms stay wrapped around my belly. "Hey," he says softly, nudging my head. "Don't be afraid, I'll be right beside you the whole time." He kisses me, encouragingly batting away my doubts. "I know what's running through that pretty little head right now, sweetheart. You will be a wonderful mother, Kaylee. I have no doubt about that. They are lucky to have you as a mom." He kisses me once more before holding his hand out once again for me. "How about we go inside so we can finally meet them?" This time I smile and take his hand.

The next few hours are a whirlwind. I'm admitted, checked, given an epidural, which I'm thankful for, and the doctor comes in to break my water. Adam has been by my side, caressing my hand the whole time. Anna made calls to Ethan and Alexis to let them know it's time.

Now we play the waiting game until they decide they are ready to make their appearance. I'm dilated to four now so hopefully they will be here soon. I'm still having mixed emotions about becoming a mother. It's going to happen whether I'm ready or not, I know, but I'm scared, happy, and nervous all at the same time. I want to be the parent that my father was with me. He was always encouraging, gentle, and supportive…I can go on all day about how wonderful he was. I want to be all those for my children and more. I'm afraid I might turn into my mother at times and that scares me. I don't ever want to neglect, abuse, or hurt my children.

I turn my head toward the love of my life, my fiancé, who is already staring at me. He reaches up and brushes away the hair that has fallen over my eyes. Adam leans forward, resting his forehead against mine. I will never get tired of him gazing into my eyes.

"Just think, sweetheart, soon we will have two babies to cherish for the rest of our lives. I bet they will look as beautiful as their mother." He kisses me passionately, making my heart beat ninety to nothing.

He pulls away, leaving a dopey grin on my face. "Thank you for sticking by me through all of this. I'd be lost without you in my life."

"I wouldn't want to be anywhere else, sweetheart."

I hear a brief knock then the door opens. Alexis walks in with Ethan right behind her. I stare at both of them, noticing something off between them. I can't put my finger on it, but something definitely happened. Alexis looks as if she has been crying and Ethan just looks pissed. Come to think of it…why are they just now getting here? I have been here going on three hours.

Alexis comes over and hugs me. "Congrats, baby girl. I can't wait to meet them!" She is now smiling, trying to pretend everything is okay. She and I are definitely having a talk later.

She steps back, letting Ethan by so he can swoop in and hug me. "Don't worry, sis. I promise not to teach them anything bad," he jokes.

We all laugh just as the nurse walks in. She asks everyone except Adam to leave so she can check me. "Good news, you are at nine! Not much longer now!" She instructs me to let the epidural wear off just a bit so it will make it easier to push when it's time. "I'll be back in about thirty minutes to recheck you." I smile warmly at her as she leaves.

Everyone returns and we all make small talk for the little bit as we anxiously wait for the next thirty minutes to tick by. Adam and I briefly discussed having his mom in the room with us when the twins were born last week. We decided we wanted it to be just us, but now I am wondering if I am going to need her with me.

"Adam," I call, getting his attention.

"Yeah, sweetheart?"

"Um, I just thought I might need your mom in here with us when it's time. I know we planned on it just being us, but I'd really like for her to be with us if that's okay." I grimace a little, feeling some of the contractions. The epidural is wearing off all right.

He squeezes my hand, grinning from ear to ear. "Of course, Kaylee. She's going to be ecstatic." He calls her over and delivers the news. Her hand flies to her mouth, obviously shocked. Tears pool in her eyes as she leans down to hug me.

"Thank you so much for this, sweetie," she gushes in my ear. She is hugging Adam as the nurse returns.

Once again, everyone but Adam leaves. "Girl, it's time. I'm going to go get the doctor!" She rushes out and Adam squeezes my hand once more.

Nerves and excitement bombard my body. I close my eyes and breathe deeply, trying to keep myself calm.

"This is it, sweetheart. I love you."

I place my hand on his cheek. "I love you so much."

"One good push and we should have baby number one," the doctor calls out. I have been pushing for an hour and my body is worn out.

"Almost there, sweetheart. You can do this," Adam coaches from beside me.

Anna is on the other side of me holding my hand. "You're doing great, sweetie," she praises.

I'm exhausted, hot, and on top of that, the epidural is practically gone. Using what little strength I have left, I scrunch my face and push, determined to get my babies out.

Cries suddenly echo throughout the room. "We have a boy!" the doctor announces and I take the moment to breathe.

Adam cuts the cord and the nurse whisks him away. From the glimpse I saw of him, he had some dark hair.

I begin the task of pushing again. A few minutes later, the sound of a baby's wailing erupts, filling the room again. "And we have a girl!"

Adam cuts the cord a second time before she is carried away.

Adam is back at my side, kissing my sweaty forehead. "You did great, Kaylee. I'm so proud of you, sweetheart," Adam croons, kissing me happily. He reaches up and brushes my sweat-soaked hair away.

"They are so precious sweetie! I'm going to let you and Adam have a few minutes alone with them while I go inform everyone they have arrived!" Anna slips out the door, heading to the waiting room.

The nurse brings Jackson to me while Adam takes Jasmine. I cradle him against my chest, admiring my baby boy. I tug his blue boggin down on his head since it was sliding off. I'm instantly in love. Who knew that such a small, tiny human being could fill your heart with joy in an instant?

My heart swells when I look over at Adam with our daughter. He is rocking her gently, talking to her sweetly. Her tiny hand is gripping his index finger. She already has him in the palm of her hand. I smile at the thought. My eyes mist at the swirl of emotions running through me. I wipe my eyes and kiss Jackson on his head. This is one of the happiest moment of my life.

Moments like this make me miss my father. I know that he is watching, smiling down at us right now. My heart plummets when I realize my kids will never know their grandfather. My dad will never get to hold them, feed them, tell them bedtime stories…nothing. He will not get to see any of their milestones or watch them grow.

The bed dips from Adam's weight as he sits on the edge of the bed. "What's the matter, sweetheart?"

I cry softly, clutching Jackson to my chest. "I wish he was here." I don't have to say my dad's name because Adam knows who I'm talking about.

"Me too, Kaylee." He cradles Jasmine in one arm while he wraps the other one around me, pulling me to him. "They will know about their grandfather and what an amazing man he was, I promise you." Tears fall freely down my cheeks. I'm so lucky to have Adam in my life.

We swap babies so I can hold Jasmine for a minute before everyone barges in and snatches them away from us.

As suspected, a couple of minutes later the door bursts open as they all fight their way through, arguing over who gets to hold them first. The grandparents win, of course. I kiss Jasmine and hand her off to Anna while Jack takes Jackson from Adam. Jack and Anna stand at the end of the bed, admiring their newborn grandchildren while Ethan and Alexis crowd around on each side, looking on in awe.

I lean into Adam's chest and sigh happily. "I love you, Lucas Adam Thomas."

He leans down and kisses me profoundly. "And I love you, Kaylee Annabel Harper."

My heart is so full right now. Never in a million years did I think I would feel this way again.

It goes to show that no matter how hard life knocks you down, you can always stand again.

## Adam

*"My heart is so full right now, watching Kaylee with Jackson and Jasmine."- Adam*

I sit in the recliner rocking Jasmine, who is currently sound asleep against my chest with her tiny hand wrapped around my index finger. She is so beautiful, just like her momma. Both Jackson and Jasmine look exactly like Riley. No lie, they are the spitting image of him. I'm not sure how I feel about that, honestly, but I'm not going to dwell on it. All that matters is that they are healthy.

Both came out with heads full of dark hair. Thank goodness, they are not the same gender or we would have problems telling them apart.

Kaylee walks back in the living room carrying Jackson in her arms. The hospital discharged us a week ago. Thank goodness, we only had to stay at the hospital for two days. I hardly got any sleep because the pullout bed was hard. I ended up sharing the bed with Kaylee, which was ten times better.

The twins actually sleep pretty well. They only wake up at one and four in the morning right now.

I move over so Kaylee can sit next to me. She sits down and lays her head on my shoulder. "Who knew that someone so tiny can steal your heart so fast?" Kaylee murmurs, smiling down at Jackson.

"You stole my heart pretty fast, sweetheart," I tell her.

"And I won't ever give it back."

I kiss her forehead. "Good, I want you to keep it forever."

The front door swings open, ruining our moment. Brad and Alexis come in and immediately swipe Jackson and Jasmine from us.

"Hey, beautiful," Alexis croons to Jasmine. Come to think of it, I don't think Kaylee and I ever told her Jasmine's middle name.

"Alexis, you know what Jasmine's middle name is, don't you?" I ask.

"No, what is it?" she asks, not taking her eyes off my daughter.

I look at Kaylee and smile. I'm going to let her be the one to tell Alexis.

"Her full name is Jasmine Alexis Thomas," Kaylee says.

Alexis whips her head around to us. "Really?!"

"Yeah, why would I tell you and it not be true?"

Alexis narrows her eyes at me. "I wasn't asking you."

"I wanted to name her after my best friend, who is more like a sister to me. You have been by my side through everything, Alexis."

I see tears form in Alexis' eyes as she walks over to hug Kaylee. "Thank you," she says in her ear.

Finally, Ethan arrives looking half-asleep. He has been working the night shift ever since the police department hired him. As far as I know, he loves his job.

"Where are my niece and nephew at?" he asks as he closes the front door behind him. Brad hands Jackson to him willingly. "Hey, now, don't be hogging her," he says when Alexis refuses to give up Jasmine.

"Are you going to be able to hold both of them at once?" Alexis sneers at him, holding Jasmine's head against her chest.

"I cradle both of them in my arms every time I see them so, yes, I can. It's not like they are huge. These little boogers are tiny, Lex."

Alexis ignores him and reluctantly hands Jasmine over to Ethan, who cradles her in his free arm. She then moves to sit on Brad's lap so Ethan can have a place to sit.

I slink my arm around Kaylee's shoulders, pulling her to my side. She curls closer, her arm wrapping around my middle. Kaylee and I usually lay in bed at night with my arm wrapped around her and the twins laying on her chest. I know we are spoiling the heck out of them, but it's tough not to want to hold them constantly.

I love watching Kaylee with Jackson and Jasmine; being a mother comes naturally for her. I understand why she had doubts, but she seems to have taken a lot after her father.

Kaylee and I have been talking about asking Ethan and Alexis to be Jackson and Jasmine's godparents. We are both for it; we just have to ask them if they are okay with it. God forbid something ever happens to us, we want them to be the ones to take care of our children. Mom and Dad are in their forties, and I know they would take care of Jackson and Jasmine in a heartbeat, but I don't want to put them in that position.

"Ethan, Alexis, can Adam and I talk to you for a second?" Kaylee asks nervously.

I don't foresee them saying no, but Ethan may take some convincing.

Ethan and Alexis exchange glances. "What's up, baby girl?"

"Well, Adam and I have been thinking—"

"Oh hell, that can never be good!" Ethan bellows.

Alexis smacks his arm. "Shut up and let her talk!"

He just glares at her before turning his attention back to Kaylee. "Sorry sis, you were saying?"

Kaylee just rolls her eyes at him. "Anyway…before I was rudely interrupted…Adam and I have been talking and we would like to make you two Jackson and Jasmine's godparents."

Alexis jumps up from Brad's lap and starts squealing. I have to plug my ears to muffle some of her yelling. Ethan just sits there, looking unsure. I wasn't sure if he would or not. It's not because he doesn't love Jackson and Jasmine, it's because of his career. Being in the military is keeping him from looking into the future.

"I'm honored sis, I really am, but you know what I do. My job is not for the faint of heart. You know what can happen."

"But you're my brother and their uncle. If you don't want to, I'll understand, but I really hope you think about it," she pleads. This is really crushing Kaylee. I had Brad in mind if Ethan declined, but for Kaylee's sake, I hope he chooses to.

"Ethan, one of us could walk out that door and never return. I get that your job puts you at a higher risk but be a real man. You love Jackson and Jasmine, so why not?" I question him.

"I do love them like they're my own."

"Hey, now, let's not get carried away," I joke.

Ethan smiles. "Okay, I accept. I'll be their godparent."

"Good, now that we have that established, can I have my son and daughter back now? We'd like to love on them some more before Mom and Dad come home and steal them from us."

Humor lights up his face. "I'll think about it."

Kaylee surprises me by getting up and hitting him in the back of his head. He sighs and gives up Jackson first. Once Jackson is content in my arms, she goes back for Jasmine.

Ethan rubs the back of his head where Kaylee slapped him. "Dang, sis. You didn't have to hit me that hard."

"Serves you right," she fires back.

Later that evening, Kaylee, the twins, and I are in the middle of our late night routine. After we have bathed and fed them, we all curl up and Kaylee and I each take turns reading them a story, even though they sleep through half the story sometimes.

Nighttime is my favorite because we are all together.

I turn to Kaylee, drinking in her beauty. "I love you, sweetheart."

She smiles sweetly at me. "I love you more."

"Impossible."

She leans toward me, pressing her lips to mine. I groan in appreciation. Kaylee is more than what I could've ever asked for. I remind her every day how much I love her, Jackson, and Jasmine.

All three of them are my world, my life.

# Epilogue

## Kaylee

Sand between my toes, a slight breeze blowing, and the sun beating down on us—it was a perfect day. Each moment in my life, whether it be sad, heartbreaking, or happy, brought me to this moment, right now.

In front to my left, I spot Anna and Jack with our three-month-old babies. Each day with them is amazing even with the few sleepless nights Adam and I endure. My fears of being a mom vanished the moment they were born. Every coo, every noise, heck, everything they do is so adorable. Adam has been amazing, just like I knew he'd be.

A couple of feet in front of them, Alexis, my best friend, my sister, stands with a beaming smile in her hot pink dress. I seriously don't know what I'd do without her. She has helped me so much over the years, I know that if we had not been paired together to work on the project, I wouldn't have had the luxury of knowing what having someone you can always count on feels like. Nor would I have had a phone, laptop, or anything. I'm so grateful and blessed to have her.

By my side is my brother, the closest thing to my father I have left. Ethan and I were blessed to look like our father. After reuniting almost a year ago, he is now also my best friend. Growing up alone sucked since it left me with no one to cope with after losing Dad. Dad was right; Ethan and I have the best relationship siblings should have.

My breath catches at the sight of Adam standing before me with Brad, his best friend, to his left. My mouth goes dry at the sight of him standing there in a white button up shirt and khakis.

My eyes never leaving his, I fight the urge to run and jump in his arms. His arms are relaxed by his side, and his breathtaking smile adorns his beautiful face.

Today is the day I will marry the love of my life. Today is the day I officially become Mrs. Lucas Adam Thomas. My dad's letter is tucked safely in my bra; my something old. My white sundress is my something new. The bracelet that is on my wrist is my something borrowed. Anna wore it the day she married Jack. My something blue is my garter that my soon-to-be husband will get to take off later.

A lone chair to my left holds an eight-by-ten framed picture of my father. I wanted him to be here with us. I smile when I think about the tattoo I got three weeks ago. On my right shoulder blade, I had the words "Daddy's Girl" inscribed with angel wings on each end. The left wing holds the year he was born and the right wing holds the year I lost him.

I slow to a stop in front of Adam, drinking him in.

I drop my hand from Ethan's elbow and turn, hugging him hard.

I zone out the minister, focusing only on Adam. Not once did I believe my heart would ever completely heal. I assumed there would still be pieces missing, but I was wrong. Standing here with my hands entwined with his, I realize that Adam picked up the pieces to my heart and put them back in place. Because of him, I finally came to terms with my father's death. Because of him, my broken heart has been healed.

Looking up at the sky, I close my eyes and mouth "I love you" to my dad before turning my attention back to my future, my forever.

*The End*

## Author Biography

Shelby lives in Sweet Home Alabama with her amazing husband and their energetic son. When she is not plotting out stories, penning chapters, or working her part-time job, you can find Shelby spending time with her family and friends, reading, and watching reruns of One Tree Hill. Shelby is obsessed with Harry Potter and Alabama Football. Roll Tide.

Shelby writes Young Adult and New Adult romance. Her characters go through tough times, get in fights, and get their hearts broken, but in the end they will live happily ever after.

## Books by Shelby

Pieces Series:

Picking up the Pieces


## Upcoming Releases

Safe with You (Saved #1) - August 2015

Torn into Pieces (Pieces #3) – Fall 2015

Made in the USA
Charleston, SC
08 June 2015